Peel's Holiday

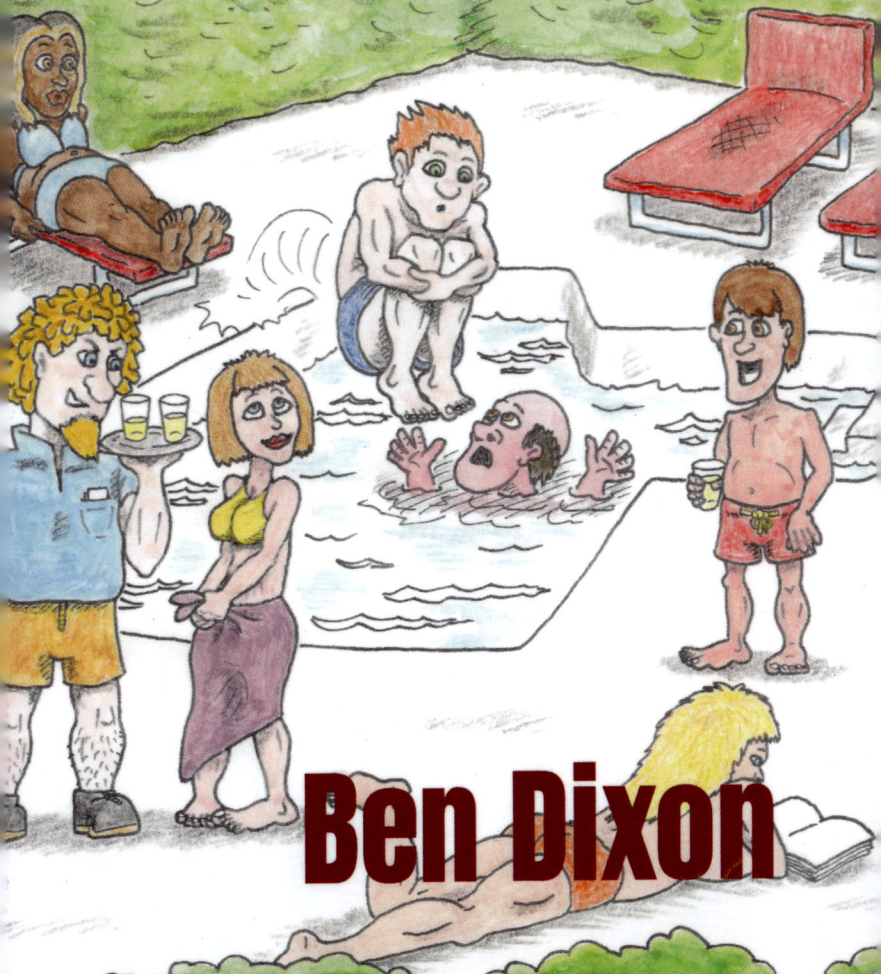

Ben Dixon

Neil Peel's Holiday

Ben Dixon

To my mum, Pat Dixon, who always inspired and encouraged me. I know you're still smiling down on me.

CONTENTS

ACKNOWLEDGMENTS

I would like to thank Sophie Dixon, Isabelle Dixon, Max Dixon and Sarah Green for reading this and helping me to tone down the content to just-about-acceptable.

Thanks again to Simon Green for his wonderful cover design!

Robin and Pat Dixon have been the most supportive parents at every stage of the journey. I can't thank you enough.

Finally, sincere thanks to everybody who has said or written kind words to me after reading my books. That makes the whole process worthwhile.

CHAPTER 1

WILBERFORCE BE WITH YOU?

My friends were all trapped, in deadly peril. I, Neil Peel, was their only hope, and I had to do something fast. There was a discarded axe on the ground about five feet away from me. I knew I'd have to be stealthy, but I was confident I could reach it without making a sound. I intended to pick it up quietly and bury it in the Captain's back. Now was not the time for chickening out; it was kill or be killed, and I was going to put him down once and for all. There would almost certainly be blood, a lot of blood, yet I couldn't let that bother me. Killing this man with that axe was our only hope, my last throw of the dice.

"Go on then, Neil. Get on with it and throw the dice," said Grub, pushing his glasses back up the bridge of his nose. He peered at me expectantly over his Game Master's screen, ready to reveal the outcome of my attack. Stephen, Cameron and Wilberforce looked on as I rolled the twenty-sided die. It landed on a 15. Was that enough?

"Captain Snake Eyes doesn't even have time to turn

around before the stealthy Half-Elf, Hendel, plants the axe deep into the side of his neck. Blood jets out from his arteries and sprays across the whole cabin. His head is only loosely attached by a flap of tissue, and it flops grotesquely to one side, revealing his severed windpipe among the sinew as he falls to the floor. He is, needless to say, dead."

Grub may have been small, skinny, short-sighted and a coward in real life, but his role-playing adventures were always psychotically vivid, almost to a worrying degree. Even a simple fireball spell would usually be accompanied by an imitation of the victim's screams as well as a full description of the sulphurous smell of the burning flesh.

I'd been friends with Stephen Prince practically since birth because our dads were great friends too. He was more physically mature than the rest of us at age twelve and was getting increasingly keen on girls, saying that his curly, ginger hair and freckles were just what the ladies loved. Cameron Dufresne had saved our bacon on more than one occasion last school year, and spending time without him didn't seem right any more. The new addition to our friendship group and our Dungeons and Dragons adventure, the overweight Wilberforce Pudge, was hosting today's final instalment of The Sinister Secret of Saltmarsh. He had taken over a character of mine that my mean older sister, Lemony, had sabotaged. She'd changed his name to Geoffrey Pantsniffer and made him into a pathetic adventurer with no abilities or charisma. We had boosted Geoffrey back up a bit, but Wilberforce, being an underdog himself, enjoyed playing his character as such.

Grub insisted that we all roll for a dexterity test to see if we could avoid slipping in the dead Captain's blood. Stephen, Cameron, and I all passed the test, but Wilberforce rolled a zero and so Geoffrey had to spend two rounds unconscious after tumbling and banging his head on a treasure chest. We all found this highly amusing.

Our game reached a conclusion, and Grub read out how the experience points and treasure should be divided up. I observed as Wilberforce reached over and took an iced bun from Grub's plate while he was busy concentrating. Wilberforce's Mum, Mrs Pudge, always gave us explorers plenty of rations to keep us going through the game when we played at their house. Today it had been two sticky buns each. Wilberforce had finished his own and had started on Grub's untouched cakes, already having finished the first a few minutes earlier. I'm sure Grub knew what happened to his snacks, but he never seemed to mind.

It was still the first week of the summer holidays and only really about a week since we had all come together to trick bullies, Basher Walker and his sidekick Batesy. They had picked on us for most of our first year at Titfield School, but once they'd tried to get Wilberforce involved in committing a crime with them, we had stepped in and put a stop to their antics. We were living freely now. There was no pressure from school, it was about to be my birthday, and I would be going on holiday with my family and my best friend Stephen in just over a fortnight. Life was good.

We finished off adjusting our character sheets, congratulating Grub on his mastery of the game. Cameron admitted that he had enjoyed his first adventure so much that he couldn't wait for the next one. I was hoping for the same reaction from Wilberforce since it was his first time playing the game too; the game was much better with five players rather than three. However, I noticed that he had gone quiet and wasn't upgrading his character.

"What's the matter, Wilberforce?" I asked. Stephen, Cameron, and Grub followed my gaze too. After a moment, he gathered himself to make an announcement.

"We're moving house," he replied. "My dad got a job at a private school called Eightoaks down in the South. Head of Department. We get a house on site, and I can go to the school."

He looked downcast at having to tell us.

"Mate, why didn't you say something?" asked Stephen.

"I didn't want to spoil anything," he continued as we listened in silence. "You've been such good friends to me, and we finally got the bullies to leave us alone. This has been the best time in my life. I don't want to leave. It's taken me so long to find good friends, and now I'll have to start all over again."

None of us could quite believe it.

"I can't quite believe it," said Grub.

"We can still stay in touch though, can't we?" added Wilberforce. "It's a traditional boarding school, and they have letter-writing sessions every Sunday morning. I'll write to you guys as often as I can. Will you write back?"

"Of course," answered Grub.

"Course, mate," said Stephen.

"Sure," replied Cameron.

"Probably not," I said.

"Neil!" cried Stephen, turning to face me, his freckled face reddening to match his mop of untidy ginger hair. "What do you mean?"

"Well I'm rubbish at that sort of thing. I never get around to writing thank you notes after birthdays and Christmases, and I'm just letting Wilberforce know. It's the truth."

Honesty: my strength and my curse.

Stephen was about to have a go at me when Wilberforce laughed.

"It's all right, Stephen," he said. "He's only being honest. Who writes letters in this day and age anyway? I hope we'll be able to come back during the holidays every now and then though, and we can meet up."

"That's a definite 'yes' from me," I replied, and the mood lightened.

We stayed longer than we would usually have done to reminisce over the events of the school year and, in particular, our triumph of last week. When we finally decided to head back home, Mrs Pudge saw us to the door, cried a little and thanked us for being such good friends to her son.

"It's weird to think that he won't be here anymore after we get back from Majorca," said Stephen as we wandered back home through Lower Piercing, our village.

"True," I answered. "But at least we've still got a couple of weeks, and he's coming to my birthday party."

"Let's just make the most of the time we've got left together," said Cameron.

We all agreed on that.

CHAPTER 2

School Report

"Neil! Lemony! The post's here. Your school reports," called Mum from the bottom of the stairs.

I was just in the middle of solving my Rubik's cube, which was not easy since my diabolic little cousin, Nicolae, had rearranged all of the coloured stickers at Christmas time. I gave the last few twists before heading downstairs to see what my teachers had written about me.

Some people would be terrified of their parents seeing their school reports, but I was quite confident that I'd done as well as possible this year. Whatever Lemony might have achieved was a mystery to me; she'd always had decent if not spectacular reports before, but I suspected that she felt an element of competition now that we were both attending the same secondary school.

She was already in the kitchen and had taken one end of the table with Mum, which left me to sit beside my dad at the other end.

"Come on then, Neil. I'm sure it's a belter," said Dad, opening the envelope and sliding out the report from within.

"Okay. Let's start with the form report from Mrs Deanus. *Blah blah blah, Neil is a friendly, well-meaning boy who is fiercely loyal to his friends. In fact, they are always together and are rarely seen without smiles on their faeces…* Faeces? Smiles on your faeces, Neil! Oops. That one got through the spell checks, Mrs Deanus," chuckled Dad.

Smiling faeces made me think immediately of the smiling poo cushion nicknamed *Happy Crappy* that Lemony had on her bed. While Dad was finding the next subject report to read, my attention wandered to the other side of the table where Mum was probably having a tough time with Lemony.

"*English, A1, Lemony always gives of her best and uses varied and vivid vocabulary in her descriptions.* Well done, darling. *Science, A1, Lemony takes great care with her written reports and works well with a partner during experiments.* Oh, this is super!"

What was this? Top grades were one thing, but working well with a partner? Was this really Lemony's report, or had they sent somebody else's by accident? My sister was listening casually as if she knew what was coming. There was a half-smile on her lips, and I sensed that she was also paying attention to what Dad was reading about me at the same time.

"*English, C3,*" continued Dad. "*Neil struggles with the creative element of this subject. He does not find it easy to invent stories that are not necessarily true and may be eligible for some kind of support in the future…*Eligible for a good shoeing more like. You manage to manipulate the truth in those role-playing games, so do the same in your English lessons."

I nodded but was still really listening to Mum.

"*Religion and Ethics, A1, Lemony shows remarkable empathy to the plight of those in suffering around the world. Her understanding of right and wrong is exceptional.*"

What was this nonsense?

"Oh, I'm so proud of you, dear. *PE, E5.* E5? That's a bit of a dip," added Mum before reading the description. *"Lemony makes no effort at all and does everything she can to avoid taking part. Sitting down does not count as sport, and I do not believe she has arthritis in her left knee which only flares up between 11.10 and 11.55 on Thursdays."*

Lemony smiled as if this were her best report. "Yes, well Mr Ashley is a total dingus who doesn't respect me at all. You can tell he's just been bluffing his way through teaching for years. He shouldn't be in the job if you ask me."

"French, B1," read Dad. *"Neil has made great progress with his French. He is not a natural linguist, but he really wants to impress.* On-ee-on. Good effort, Neil. French is definitely the language if you want to woo ze ladies."

This comment of Dad's was not too far off the mark. I had been trying particularly hard in French lessons because of the beautiful, serene Fleur Poucette who sat just behind me. Her wavy blonde hair and pale blue eyes had mesmerised me, although I wasn't quite sure how to go about mesmerising her in return.

"History, B2," continued Dad. *"At the start of the year, Neil was quick to point out the factual mistakes of his classmates, but lately he has made so much progress that he's almost become invisible.* Become invisible? Is that a good thing?"

The longer this went on, the more predictable it became. Lemony was barely even acknowledging the top grades she was getting, and the two A1 grades I'd got for Maths and Science seemed to pale in comparison with her almost perfect report. Then came my PE report; my big chance to outperform my sister.

"PE, D2," said Dad. *"Neil should be commended for trying in his PE lessons, but he lacks the elementary coordination needed to succeed. Perhaps he could practise some basic throwing and catching skills over the holidays."*

Well that was a bit harsh, and I was probably in

agreement with Lemony that Mr Ashley was being a dingus, whatever one of those was. However, while his remarks were sinking in, I noticed that Lemony was looking at Dad and smiling to herself. Even though I had a better grade than her, the comment about me was more insulting because I'd tried but not managed to achieve much, whereas Lemony clearly hadn't bothered at all.

Finally, Mum and Dad got to the end of our reports. Mum almost didn't notice that Lemony had earned a special Headmistress's commendation from Mrs Rees for her outstanding improvement.

"How was Neil's report?" asked Mum, glancing over.

"Fine. Yes. Good," answered Dad, pushing my report over for Mum to read. "The boy's made a solid start. How about Lemony?"

"Well, it's amazing," said Mum. "Truly amazing. Last year, the teachers almost all said she was disengaged but clever; this year, it's A1 for everything except PE! The girl's a genius. And listen to this. Mrs Rees has put a commendation slip in too. It says: *Congratulations to the following three year ten girls: Ophelia Bishop and Anais Bowl for raising £300 by volunteering to cut off eight inches…*"

"Sounds painful," interrupted Dad with a grin and a raise of his eyebrows.

"*…eight inches of their hair for charity,*" resumed Mum with building emotion, "*and to Lemony Peel for her outstanding improvement and for having the best academic report in the year group.*"

"It's no big deal," said Lemony, standing up and walking around the table nonchalantly. "Doing well at school is just a matter of catching what they throw at you. You know. Jumping through hoops. Anyone can do it if you're willing to be a slave to the grind."

That comment was clearly a dig at my PE report, and I was a little exasperated. My report hadn't been bad at all, but my sister had a way of making me feel inadequate, and she was relishing it without saying anything directly. Her point was proven, and I was almost sure that she would slip back into mediocracy next year.

"I'm going into Lowcester shopping with Ella," announced Lemony. "We need to get new swimwear for the holiday, and nothing's cheap."

"Oh, yes dear," said Mum, catching Lemony's meaning and reaching for her purse. "Have you got twenty quid, John? I've only got thirty for our little genius."

Dad found the requisite extra, and Lemony bounced out of the kitchen, glancing at me expressionlessly on the way through, and out through the front door. Mum had gone back to my report and was frowning, mumbling quizzically about *smiling faeces*.

"Don't worry, Neil," consoled Dad. "Yours is good too. They never over-grade in the first year. Just look at me. I got a C for Art in my GCSE, and now I work for one of the top three architectural design companies in Lowcester."

"But Dad," I replied. "There are only three architectural design companies in Lowcester, and anyway, you're their accountant."

"Exactly my point," answered Dad. "One of the top three. And we make nearly as much profit as the other two. Oh, by the way," he added as an afterthought, "do you want to go and chuck a ball around in the park?"

"No thanks, Dad," I groaned. "We're all going to Stephen's house to watch a film later."

Mum looked up from my report, trying to mask the jolt back to reality she was having after having read of Lemony's successes.

"But Stephen's mum and dad are coming round to talk about the holiday," she said, looking disappointed. "We thought it would be nice to discuss it all together. Now Lemony's gone out, and you'll be round at their house while they're over here."

"Sorry, Mum," I answered. "We need to spend as much time as possible with Wilberforce before he moves away.

Anyway, if Stephen's dad is anything to go by, the holiday plans will involve sitting by the pool every day and making full use of the all-inclusive booze."

"Cheers to that!" added Dad, raising his cup of tea in salute.

"Come on, John," reprimanded Mum while leafing through the *Explore Majorca* book that was also on the table. "There are some lovely places to visit in Majorca. Some nice walks in the hills, and you can find some secluded pools and waterfalls, apparently."

"Well, if they do a Blue Lagoon cocktail at the pool bar, I'll dive right into that," joked Dad. "Anyway, Mike and Diana have been going back to Cala Plata every year for ages, so they know it like the back of their hands."

I considered this to be a good time to slip away.

CHAPTER 3

FILM NIGHT

Sure enough, just as I arrived at Stephen's house and was about to knock, film and snack bag in hand, Mike and Diana Prince opened the front door and smiled at me. I knew them very well since my dad and Mike Prince had been best friends forever. Even so, I still called them Mr and Mrs Prince, and Stephen still called my parents Mr and Mrs Peel. Mike was a jolly, fat man who always had a quip for every occasion. He and Diana were very relaxed about what Stephen did and when he could go out, so I wondered how that would work in Majorca; I would be sharing an apartment with Stephen, Mike and Diana while Mum, Dad, Lemony and her friend Ella Umber were going to be in the apartment next door.

Mike had receding, short-cropped dark hair, in contrast to Diana who was pale and had light strawberry-blonde hair. That combination must have been perfect to produce Stephen whose pale complexion and ginger hair meant that he and his mum would definitely be sharing the factor 50 on holiday.

"Hello, Neil. The others are already here," said Diana, pulling me into a one-armed hug. She actually has two arms, but she was holding her handbag in one, so she just used the other.

"Hey, Neil," chuckled Mike before squeezing my shoulder. "Been working on the beach body, have you? I know I have. Check out this for a six-pack."

Rather predictably, he pretended he was about to raise his shirt but then pulled a small crate of beer from behind his back and burst out laughing.

"Nice one, Mr Prince," I said, laughing politely. "Are you going to tell my dad the same joke when you get round to our house?"

"Of course he will!" cried Diana before letting go her trademark machine gun laugh.

"Too right," continued Mike. "You've got to share the good ones. Come on then, love. See you later, Neil. The boys seem to have plenty of snacks and pop."

"What's pop?" I asked quietly as they wandered out of the drive without hearing me.

*

"What's up, brother from another mother?" yelled Stephen from the lounge. He was sitting lodged in a huge cardboard box that must have contained some item of delivered furniture. This didn't seem odd to me at all because it was Stephen, and that was the kind of thing he did. Wilberforce and Cameron were in the two easy chairs while Grub was reclining on a bean bag in front of the television.

"Hey, Neil," they all added.

"Stephen's just been telling us all about what you're going to be getting up to on holiday," said Cameron. "Sounds lively."

Stephen crawled out of his box and leapt to his feet on

the sofa, adopting a surfing pose.

"True," he enthused. "Watch out, Majorcan girls. The Peel-Prince love machine is about to take Cala Plata by storm!"

"I'm not sure about that," I replied, sitting down next to Stephen, "but I am really looking forward to it. The sea should be warm, and the resort's pool is huge."

"Well, make sure you wear goggles in the pool," advised Grub. "You don't want to get PPI."

"What are you talking about, Grub?" asked Stephen.

"You must have heard about people getting PPI checks. It's all over the TV and radio," said Grub, sounding authoritative. "And people pee in the swimming pool all the time, so wear goggles and it won't get in your eyes. No PPI."

I was sure that Grub had made another mistake and that PPI was something to do with money rather than getting urine in your eyes, but I couldn't speak with certainty, so I changed the subject.

"Are you guys going away?"

"My parents are going to be too busy with the move for a holiday this year," answered Wilberforce.

"Too bad," replied Grub. "We're off to Jordan. Apparently, it's forty degrees out there at the moment."

"Jordan?" asked Stephen. "Is that a real place? Are you sure your dad doesn't just have a mate called Jordan, and you're going round to his house for a barbecue?"

"No. It is a real country, Stephen," teased Grub. "It's in the Middle East."

"Do we believe him, boys?" continued Stephen. "It's like last year all over again. Where did you say you went then?"

"Tunisia," answered Grub. "Again, a real country."

"You might as well just say Tatooine, mate," concluded Stephen. "They're both equally likely to exist in my mind."

Cameron's mother was Scottish, so he was heading up to their family home on the Isle of Iona. Apparently, it was a tiny island where you weren't allowed to take cars. Weird. The thought of cars got me thinking about my birthday party.

"Is everybody excited for karting on Saturday?" I asked.

"You'd better believe it," answered Stephen immediately.

"Can't wait," added Cameron.

"Are the karts adult size?" asked Wilberforce, grinning and patting his tummy, although there was a note of genuine concern in his voice.

"One size fits all," I replied. "You just slide the seat back or forward. It was plenty big enough for my dad when we went before."

"I hope the helmets are big enough to go over my glasses?" giggled Grub nervously.

"No worries, Grub-man," I replied. "Last time, mine was too loose, so I had to get it tightened. Oh. One other thing about Saturday. They do these races in groups of ten, and there are only five of us, so there'll be another group racing with us. The lady at the kart centre said that they'd put us in a red and a green group though, so we can just compare amongst ourselves. That's good because adults get very competitive about driving."

"Anyway," announced Stephen. "Who's ready for a film? What have we all brought?"

"I wasn't sure, so I just brought extra snacks," said Wilberforce, grabbing his goodie bag.

"I've got super heroes," I said. "Marvel, DC, the lot."

"You can't go wrong with Star Wars, so I brought all of them," added Grub while bumping his fist to mine to salute my film choices. "Fish bump," he said.

"*Fish* bump?" questioned Stephen. "Is this another Grub classic? Oh yes."

Grub flushed scarlet, embarrassed at his gaff.

"You *bump* your *fist* against someone else's. Why on Earth would it be a *fish* bump?" asked Stephen.

15

"All right, all right," said Grub, looking around for a way out of the conversation.

"Back to the Future trilogy and some other eighties classics here," offered Cameron, holding up his backpack.

"Do any of those eighties classics have Molly Ringwald in by any chance?" asked Stephen with a wink.

"Don't start that again," ordered Grub.

"Who's Molly Ringwald?" asked Wilberforce.

"He does this every time," I answered. "She was a red-haired, eighties film star."

"I don't see what's wrong with watching something with a strong, ginger role-model. If she happens to be hot as well then that's an added bonus," said Stephen with a smile. "And it is my house after all."

Grub had had enough.

"No Molly Ringwald. No Nicole Kidman. No Lindsay Lohan and definitely no Little Orphan Annie. I'm still not sure how you got us to watch the Little Mermaid last time."

Stephen threw back his head and laughed. "How about the Lorax?"

We all burst out laughing at that, although someone started pelting Stephen with popcorn, and we all joined in. Once we'd cleared up the mess, we carried on the discussion.

"I think I've got a solution," I suggested. "Avengers is something we all like, and Black Widow's a ginger. Plus, Iron Man's head is mostly red too."

"Interesting idea," pondered Stephen. "I could wear my Iron Man mask at the same time."

His voice-altering Iron Man mask had proven very useful in our campaign against Basher Walker and Batesy earlier in the summer, even if I'd only discovered that the batteries were failing at the crucial moment in our plan to disguise my voice.

"But I only saw that last week," protested Grub. "Let's have a look at Cameron's eighties films. Perhaps there's something we haven't seen before."

And so the discussion continued for another half hour before we finally agreed on something. Well, all of us except Grub anyway.

Ninety minutes later, after the film had finished, we parted ways, and I headed home singing *Under the Sea* to myself. Stephen could be very persuasive when he wanted.

CHAPTER 4

MY BIRTHDAY PARTY

Saturday was a dull, overcast day, but it didn't matter to me. It was my birthday! I was now twelve years old. The problem with having a birthday on 12th July is that nearly everybody in your school year has had their birthday at some point already. I was one of the only three out of my class of twenty-seven who was still eleven at the end of term.

I didn't bound down the stairs as I used to do on my birthdays when I was younger, nor did I wake up ridiculously early, but it was still pretty exciting. I wanted to go in and see if Mum and Dad were up, but I had to do a check on their door first.

Usually, they slept with the door ajar, but at the weekends I would often get up to find it closed. Dad seemed to have a workout routine that he would save until first thing in the mornings at the weekend, and I could occasionally hear Mum giggling. A bit later, they would both go to the toilet in their en suite bathroom, and then

Mum would have a shower, singing to herself, which she never usually did. Dad would come down to make a cup of tea, pretty red in the face after his workout, and that was the sign that their day could begin. For some reason, Lemony had told me that I was being naïve if I thought they weren't 'playing games for mummies and daddies', but she was just being mean again. After all, they had finished having children, so her theory made no sense.

Tying my Darth Vader dressing gown around my waist, I spotted that the door was wide open this morning, and Mum and Dad were not in their bedroom at all. My stomach rumbled at a familiar odour, so I followed my nose downstairs, noticing lots of coloured balloons scattered around the lounge as I went past the doorway. I moved through to the kitchen to find my parents both having a cup of tea. The radio was on quietly while Dad was making his American pancakes with blueberries and fried bananas, and Mum was still poring over the *Explore Majorca* handbook. She looked up as I entered and cried out, "Here he is. Happy birthday, sweetheart!"

"Thanks, Mum," I smiled, accepting her hearty hug.

"Happy birthday, champ," added Dad, ruffling my hair and hugging me too. "Ready for some pancakes?"

I certainly was and devoured five of the delicious little discs in no time at all, smothering them in maple syrup to make them even tastier. After washing them down with a glass of fresh orange juice, I was led by the hand into the lounge for presents.

"There aren't as many in here as usual because you'll be seeing everybody else tomorrow at the family gathering," said Mum, settling down by the small pile of presents next to the fireplace. I had to boot a balloon out of the way and kicked it again as it was landing. It fell close to me, so I kneed it a third time. Eat your heart out, Mr Ashley. Who said I was lacking coordination? A boy in my class, Vijay Jayasuriya, had claimed that he had once done a thousand keepy-uppies with a balloon before getting bored. I hadn't believed him but wondered whether I might have a go at that later on.

Once Dad had come in too, Mum handed me the first present. Something soft. I savoured the feeling for a fraction of a second before tearing open the paper. It was a thick, dark green Avengers hoodie with a black 'A' logo on the front.

"Thanks," I said. "I'll definitely be wearing that for karting today, even if it is summer."

In the next batch were some books for the flight and by the pool on holiday. Among them was the latest one by my favourite author, Frank Beans, who wrote funny stories. They were probably aimed at people a bit younger than twelve as they had quite a few illustrations, and the words were really spread out on the page, but they never failed to make me laugh. Anyway, there weren't many funny books around for slightly older children. Someone should fill that gap in the market.

I also got some graphic novels and some original X-Men comics from the eighties. I hugged Mum and Dad to thank them for the presents.

Just then, Lemony entered the lounge with a cylindrical-shaped cardboard package in her hands. Sure, she hadn't gone to the effort of wrapping it, but at least it looked like she'd got me a present. I was wary.

"Happy birthday, younger brother," she said.

It was hard to read her expression. Usually, she would either have got me a joke present, which would have brought a sneer to the corner of her mouth, or else Mum and Dad would have bought something for her to give to me, in which case she would look as bored as ever. What was going on?

"Thanks, Lemony," I replied, noting her concern as she handed over the present.

I began to pick at the end of the tube to open it.

"Be careful!" she snapped, half reaching over to me. "You might tear the corner."

I slowed down, intrigued by what might be inside. Once I'd got the plastic end off, I slid out the contents: a poster.

"Oh, Lemony. How thoughtful," said Mum, stretching over to pat her on the shoulder.

There had to be a catch. Then, as I unrolled the poster, the penny dropped. It was a poster advertising the new album, *Work out in my Sexual Gymnasium* by Durty Dreamz, Lemony's favourite band.

"Aah. Where are you going to hang it, Neil?" asked Mum.

"I'm not," I answered. "I don't even like Durty Dreamz."

"Well, if you're going to be that ungrateful, I might as well keep it," barked Lemony before taking the poster from me and marching back upstairs. I couldn't see her face, but I would bet anything that she was smiling.

*

The Lowcester Karting Centre was on an industrial estate on our side of the town. From the outside it looked like any of the other cube-shaped business buildings around it, but once inside, it was like passing into another world. There were racing overalls, helmets and hi-tech screens displaying leader boards and instant replay highlights. The smell of rubber tyres hung thick in the air.

The boys all gave me my presents as we were signing in. I got a Half-elf lead figure and some green paints from Grub, the brand-new Saltmarsh adventure sequel from Stephen, a pack of Marvel Top Trumps and a pack of Marvel playing cards from Cameron, and Wilberforce gave me a framed photo of the five of us playing Dungeons and Dragons at his house. It was very touching, and I hoped that he had kept a copy to remind him of us too.

We got kitted out in our racing gear, and, much to Grub's relief, the helmets fitted very nicely over a pair of glasses. Having finished the safety briefing, it was almost time to make our way onto the trackside, so I decided to pass on my presents to my dad who was waiting in the viewing area. Taking the steps two at a time, I arrived at the gallery and recognised my dad's back. He was leaning on a railing next to a short, fat man. They seemed to be chatting, but both turned in my direction as I approached.

"Dad, can you look after my presents while we race?" I asked.

"Of course," he replied, swallowing nervously. "Hey, Neil. Do you recognise Mr Plank? His daughter goes to Titfield as well, and it's her birthday today too. She's in the other group that's racing with you. Ottilie's her name. Do you know her?"

"Oh no!" I cried, looking between my dad and a rather surprised Mr Plank. "That'll ruin everything."

I dumped my presents with Dad and turned to hurry back downstairs. Ottilie Plank had been my desk mate for the whole of the school year, and she and I were not on good terms. Her father, Oscar 'Plankety' Plank, whom I'd just met upstairs, had made a fortune in the local building trade, and now Ottilie felt that she was better than everybody else. This was bad.

One of the pit crew opened the door for me, and I rushed through. Karts were zooming around the track as the previous group's session was drawing to a close. Cameron, Stephen, Grub and Wilberforce were all facing me, looking sheepish. Two girls were facing them, seemingly berating them for something. I recognised the long blonde hair of Ottilie and the colourfully adorned, black braids of her best friend, Remi Solfer. Remi's mother was a traditional Nigerian woman who always gave her daughter the most fascinating hair styles. Perhaps Remi might have been more pleasant if she didn't hang around with Ottilie all of the time, but she could be quite spiteful when they were together. They followed Stephen's gaze once he'd noticed my arrival and then turned to face me.

"And here's the final member of the Sad-Acts," announced Ottilie. "Thanks for ruining my birthday party."

"I'm ruining yours?" I snapped. "We've had this booked for ages."

"Well it's a shame you don't have enough friends to fill the spaces yourself then," she sniped. "Oh, and prepare to lose because I drive my quad bike around our estate all the time, so you'll have to get used to seeing the back of my head." With that, she turned, put her helmet on showing us all the red number one on the back, and returned to her other three friends, Remi smirking at her side.

"She is *so* annoying!" I blurted out to general nods from my friends.

"Neil," said Cameron, as calmly as a Zen master. "We are all humans here. This is your birthday. You came here to enjoy it, so enjoy it. Ottilie will love it if you seem to be upset, so don't give her the pleasure. If you'd rather annoy her, smile and be happy. Just have fun karting, and let us take care of the rest."

I knew he was right. She thrived on misery, so I would refuse to give in to her.

Eventually, the previous racers finished, and we were called up towards the start. We all had a green band around our helmets and Ottilie's party all had a red band on theirs.

"Gentlemen, start your engines," announced Stephen.

"And may the best woman win," replied Ottilie, raising her arm with a flourish. She put on her helmet, scowled at me in challenge from behind her visor and took her place in the first car in the left-hand row. Her friends all took their places in order behind her. The boys ushered me to take the first car on the right, level with Ottilie, but I thought about it for a moment, patted Wilberforce on the shoulder and took my place in the last car at the back of the right-hand row. Wilberforce climbed into the first car with Stephen, Grub and Cameron taking the remaining cars. Cameron winked at me as he sat down, and I noticed Ottilie looking backwards, confused that I seemed to be cheerfully refusing the obvious challenge.

I strapped myself in and checked my kart. Two pedals, accelerator and brake. Forward and reverse gears. Battery indicator: 47%. That seemed a little low, but we would only be racing for about fifteen minutes at most. My smile wasn't visible to anybody because of the helmet, but I was excited. The lights blinked, red, red...green!

Ottilie zoomed out from her pole position on the grid and into the first corner; the girls behind her followed suit. Wilberforce put pedal to the metal and shot backwards straight into Stephen's car. Cameron, Grub and I had all imagined going forwards too, and therefore ended up squashed together in a row. This was not the start we had anticipated. Eventually, we untangled ourselves, and Cameron, Stephen, and Grub took to the circuit as Wilberforce located the forward gear. He and I got going at the back of the pack, the girls nowhere to be seen. Getting the hang of the kart was not difficult, and I soon worked out how much you had to slow down for each corner to get around it efficiently. However, we had a lot of ground to make up, and by the time I'd finished my first lap, I still couldn't see any of the red-banded helmets. The big screen announced that the fastest lap so far was Ottilie with 48 seconds, and the red team occupied the first five positions. None of the green team had managed a lap of anywhere near under a minute due to our snarl-up at the start line. As the track became more familiar, negotiating it became easier. Soon enough, I came up to a red team kart and overtook it on the inside of a corner. Wilberforce was quite far back behind me now. I turned the next corner and powered up the ramp, swerving just in time to pass Grub and one of the red team whose karts were both stuck in the tyres on the side of the track. I finished the second lap in sixth place out of ten with my lap time as third fastest behind Ottilie and Cameron. This was fun.

Towards the end of lap three, I approached Stephen and red helmet number four. They were neck and neck, and neither wanted to let the other through. They rounded a turn into the final straight but bumped against each other and both span off into the sides, leaving me to slip between the pair of them. Fourth place! Somewhere up ahead were Cameron, Remi and Ottilie.

The next few laps went by without too many incidents. It was clear that I was gaining slowly on the top group because I could see them at end of the long straights. As I completed lap six, my time showed that I was only ten seconds behind Remi in third place. Mild alarm gripped me on noticing that the battery life of my kart was now down to 23%. Had I got in a kart that hadn't been properly charged?

On the next lap, I overtook Wilberforce again and also lapped one of the red team. Stephen was somewhere fairly close behind me; I could see him as we went round a hairpin bend, and we both raised fists in salute. Even more pleasing was that he had now clocked the fastest lap with 46.5 seconds, pushing Ottilie back into second place. She was, however, still in first place overall.

Two more laps went by and my battery life was plummeting. We were coming up to the final lap, and I had only 7% left! My acceleration was still strong, but there wasn't much juice left in the tank.

All of a sudden, there was a screech of tyres from elsewhere on the circuit, and, a few seconds later, Wilberforce came driving towards me, the wrong way round the track! I swerved to the right to avoid him and then saw three stuck karts ahead with the pit crew frantically trying to free them. Just as I approached, Remi, who was back in the game, tried to drive in front of me, but I deftly rounded her kart, and she lodged herself straight back into the tyres on the other side, hitting her steering wheel in frustration about having let me through. Cameron and Ottilie had also been released but had not got their acceleration up enough to stop me zooming between them. First place!

I rounded the final corner with only one more straight to go, and I was about twenty metres clear of everyone else. I raised my fist in triumph just at the very moment my battery dropped to 0% and my kart cut out completely. All of my speed disappeared, and I juddered to an abrupt halt about fifty centimetres from the finish line. What terrible luck! Ottilie and Cameron entered the final straight and were gaining on me fast. I tried rocking my kart forward with my body to roll it over the line but to no avail.

Turning to watch the battle for first place, I desperately hoped that Cameron could win for the green team. They were level again, but Ottilie was in the left-hand lane, just as I was, and Cameron was not letting her move away into the centre of the track. There was no way for her around the obstacle that was my kart. She started to pull ahead slightly but still couldn't get far enough in front of Cameron. At the last moment, she swerved to the right in a desperate attempt to get past. I braced myself for impact as Ottilie's kart slammed into mine and shunted me over the finish line into first place. Cameron must have crossed the line a fraction of a second after I did, and then Stephen came past in third before any of the pit crew had chance to set Ottilie free from the tyres at the side. Remi came through in fourth, and Grub was close behind her. Finally, Wilberforce rounded that final corner just as Ottilie was freed, but, even though he crossed the line before her, he still had another lap or two to go, having driven the wrong way around for quite some time.

Stephen, Grub, Cameron and I gave each other high fives in celebration as we parked up our karts and waited for Wilberforce. My kart had to be pushed off the track by the pit crew who were apologising for having given me one without enough power.

Ottilie and her friends were furious and stormed over to complain about the fact that we'd cheated and that she should have won. She demanded that the whole race needed to be rerun because it wasn't fair. Unfortunately for her, the pit crew didn't see anything unfair in the race, and neither did the manager when she'd called her dad down to add his (considerable) weight and bluster to her complaint.

Wilberforce eventually crossed the finish line, so we went to congratulate him and help him out of the kart.

I could hear that Ottilie was going mental, but Cameron's wise words were still foremost in my mind. I was determined to have fun with my friends on my birthday; talking to Ottilie was not on my agenda.

"You're a total disgrace and so is this whole place!" she shouted at the manager. My peripheral vision was telling me that she was rounding on me to vent some more, so I ushered the boys towards the victory podium, not even making eye contact with her. Being ignored seemed to have vexed her even further, and she stormed out of the arena, pulling off her jumpsuit as she went, just as my dad came in from the viewing gallery to take some pictures of us.

"The girls seem to be leaving in a bit of a hurry," observed Dad, "and Ottilie got her nappy in a twist, didn't she? Her dad was a bit of a … plonker, or perhaps I mean planker? He didn't like seeing her overtaken by you all at the end. I couldn't stick watching the second race with him, so I was working on excuses. I'd narrowed it down to saying either that I'd got diarrhoea or that Gotham City needed me."

While Dad was taking photos of us on the podium with a pretend champagne bottle, wreath, and trophy, Wilberforce explained that he'd thought everyone else was driving the wrong way around the track when he'd been rescued following a crash. We were all in good spirits as we headed upstairs to the café for lunch and birthday cake. It was no surprise that Ottilie's party would not have reserved to eat up here; it would have been beneath her, but it was a very pleasant surprise that they didn't return for the next race after lunch. The manager even let my dad race free since the five girls weren't there, and they'd made an error giving me a kart without enough power. Our second session was full of fun and much more relaxed, everything a birthday party should be.

CHAPTER 5

A FAMILY BIRTHDAY

In addition to my birthday party, Mum and Dad had organised a family get-together on the following day. There was a picturesque village called Itchington Fenny that was half way between Lower Piercing and Hampton's End where Nanna and Grandpa lived, so a table had been reserved for us to have lunch. Mum had asked me to wear one of my two smart shirts for the occasion; I'd chosen the pale blue one with the vertical red stripes in the same way I made most of my fashion decisions: whichever was nearest to me when I opened the wardrobe.

As usual, the format was the same as in any Peel family drive lasting over an hour. Dad was driving, listening to rock songs, tapping on the steering wheel, and occasionally jerking his head in time with the music and humming along in a "ta-na-ta-pah" type of way. Mum was asleep, snoring from time to time then waking herself up temporarily if her head dropped suddenly. Lemony sat behind Dad, staring out of the window with a glance between us every five minutes to make sure that every part of my body was within my half of the back seat. I had no idea what was going on in her enigmatic mind, but it certainly wasn't anything that made her smile. I was behind Mum, looking out of my window and wondering about the afternoon ahead. We'd been to this particular country house restaurant once before for Nanna and Grandpa's forty-fifth wedding anniversary; my uncle Peter had come that time too, but that was in the days before he'd married Auntie Lexa and had spawned the Antichrist, Nicolae, as his child.

Today would be interesting. I hadn't parted on good terms from my uncle Peter the last time we'd been together, after Nicolae had done his best to ruin Christmas for me. To add spice to the mix, Mum had invited her sister, Auntie Sue, along for lunch. She was a lovely, cheery lady, devoutly religious and pure. If there was a polar opposite of my beer-swilling uncle, then it was Auntie Sue. I couldn't recall having ever seen them together in my recent memory, but Mum said they'd met just after I was born, and things had got tense when Peter suggested taking Dad for a 'celebratory ale' at the pub rather than spending time with his new God-given gift of a son.

I wondered if Auntie Sue would be able to spot Satan in Nicolae.

*

"Coo-ee! Neil!" called Auntie Sue enthusiastically. "There's the birthday boy! Happy Birthday. Ah. God bless you."

Having arrived at the country house and parked the car, we'd gone in to the restaurant to find that Auntie Sue had already arrived and was sitting at the table waiting for us. I went over and gave her a hug, recoiling slightly at the strong smell of lavender.

"Twelve years old?" she continued. "I can hardly

believe it, but it's been written in my Cliff Richard calendar since January, so it must be true."

She chuckled, gave me an envelope, and kissed my forehead.

"I thought that you've got everything you need," she added, "and there are people a lot worse off than you in the world, so I made a donation to Christian Aid instead of getting you a present."

"Oh, okay," I replied. "So, no present."

"Well, there is a little something in there," she said, pointing to the envelope. I opened it up and took out the card which told me how precious I was to Jesus. There was a bookmark inside but nothing else.

"Where?" I asked.

"Right there, you silly sausage!" said Auntie Sue, showing me the bookmark.

"Oh, that's it?" I said, trying not to sound disappointed.

The bookmark told me that 'Neil' means champion, that my greatest qualities are tenacity and dexterity, my lucky gemstone is emerald, my lucky number is five, and my greatest flaws are bluntness and deception.

"Well most of that is a load of…" I began.

"How was your journey, Sue?" interrupted my mum, stepping in to hug her sister and divert attention from the generic lies on the bookmark. Dad followed suit, and Mum took the envelope and slipped it into her handbag, giving me a pleading look.

"Can I get you a drink from the bar, Sue?" asked Dad. "Glass of wine, beer, triple vodka?"

"You are a tease, John," giggled Auntie Sue. "Just Adam's ale for me, please. Still rather than sparkling, with a slice of lemon if they have one. I've taken to having my libations infused with citrus at home. Can you imagine such a thing?"

Dad went to get the drinks just as everybody else arrived. Uncle Peter, Auntie Lexa and Nicolae had picked

31

up my nanna and grandpa on the way through, and there were more hugs of congratulation about my birthday as well as greetings all around. One thing that couldn't escape my notice was that my Auntie Lexa had put on a lot of weight since Christmas.

"Wow, Auntie Lexa," I exclaimed. "You're nearly as fat as Uncle Peter now."

"Peej, my good man! Liddle drinky-poos?" asked my dad of his brother. "A snifter of some beverage perhaps?

"Well I don't mind if I do," replied Uncle Peter. "That's terribly, terribly kind of you, old sport."

"Glass of wine, Sexa?" called my dad from the bar, dropping his upper-class twit voice. He always called her Sexa because he thought that was funnier than her real name of Lexa Peel.

"Not for me, John," she answered in her strong Romanian accent while wiping her runny nose on a tissue. "Just an orange juice. I need the vitamins for my cold, but you are right that I am much thicker now, Neil. I am have another baby soon."

"How long to go, Auntie Lexa?" piped up Lemony, who had temporarily escaped from Auntie Sue.

"Only two more months then Nicolae will have little brother or *seester*," she enthused.

"So that means," continued Lemony with a glint in her eye, "that seven months ago you were with us for Christmas."

"Spot on, Lemony!" cried Uncle Peter, appearing from the bar with a pint of beer in one hand and holding Nicolae's hand in the other. "The new baby was conceived in Neil's bed on the stroke of Christmas day. Wahey!"

"What?!" I cried, quivering at an image I'd really rather not have conjured. In the corner of my eye I could see Lemony stifling her laughter. "How could you? That's disgusting!"

"Oh, Peter," despaired Nanna. "Please spare us the details." She turned and presented me with another envelope which contained a card detailing how special I was and a cheque for twenty pounds.

"Thanks, Nanna. Thanks, Grandpa," I smiled, giving them each a hug in turn.

"He's growing up so much!" exclaimed Nanna. "You'll soon be bigger than all of us."

"Especially around his gut," sneered Lemony. "Some parts of the body don't stop growing. I thought it was only supposed to be the nose and ears, but Neil's belly might be another exception."

"All bought and paid for!" added Uncle Peter, reaching over to pat my tummy.

"Can we leave Neil alone on his birthday?" requested Mum, shooting a glare at Lemony. "There's nothing wrong with him."

Nanna chuckled that Grandpa had never stopped growing. "He grew taller, grew more annoying and is now growing smaller again."

Grandpa accepted the insult in the way that older male family members seem to have to do.

"Oh yes. Happy birthday from us, too," added Uncle Peter, taking a flat, A3-sized present from Auntie Lexa and passing it to me.

I shuddered, trying to forget what I'd just heard about them in my bed at Christmas by opening this present. Ripping part of the paper, I saw the Marvel logo and began to think that perhaps my uncle had got me a decent present for once. It was a Marvel calendar. In theory this should have been right up my street, but it was now mid-July, so the year was half over.

"A calendar for this year, in July?" I asked, wondering if there was some logic I was missing.

"Precisely," replied Uncle Peter. "Only half the year gone but still reduced by 75% to one pound fifty! Bargain, eh?"

"What am I supposed to do with January to June?" I asked genuinely.

"Well, you can…" Uncle Peter started to answer before becoming distracted by Nicolae who was tugging at his arm. "What is it, sunshine? Do you need the toilet?"

"No. No toilet," answered little Nicolae.

"Well, why are you holding your willy?" he pursued.

Auntie Sue gasped audibly.

"Because it's sticking up," explained Nicolae.

"Wahey!" shouted Uncle Peter again. "He's only just three, and already it's har…"

"*It's hard to dance with the devil on your back*," interrupted Auntie Sue shrilly, bursting into a loud version of Lord of the Dance to change the direction of the conversation.

"Well," said Grandpa, diffusing the situation. "I've been on my feet for at least two minutes since we got out of the car. Time to go and sit down at the table, I think. The sooner we order, the sooner we can eat, and I'm starving. We went round to our neighbour Doris's this morning. This lunch has got to be better than sucking on one of her soggy Garibaldis."

"Well you know that's all she can manage with her false teeth," replied Nanna. "Even a firm rich tea would be pushing it."

Nanna went with Grandpa, and the rest of us followed suit. The waitress came to take our order, and by the time she'd finished, Nicolae was squirming uncontrollably in his seat.

"Peter. You take him for a poo," commanded Auntie Lexa.

"Blimey, you can't even sit for five minutes and have a wet with your own brother around here," he complained before dragging Nicolae off to the Gents' and ordering another pint of beer on the way.

*

We'd been sitting at the table waiting for a good ten minutes before Uncle Peter and Nicolae returned from the toilet.

"Sorry about that. It was a toughie," explained Uncle Peter. "Oh, and Nicolae had to go too," he added, laughing at his own joke. "The bowel moves in mysterious ways, eh Susan."

Auntie Sue flushed red and tried to ignore him. The food arrived shortly afterwards, and she said a little prayer while everybody else was getting ready to tuck in.

"Give us this day our daily bread!" said Uncle Peter who was becoming a bit antagonistic now. "But what if you have a gluten-free diet?"

"Soda bread," answered Auntie Sue immediately, nodding to the bread roll in his hand. "And you don't have a gluten-free diet, do you Peter?"

One-nil.

"Speaking of bread," she continued, proudly, "I made the most delightful *Dampfnudel* last weekend. I'd seen it on that baking show and thought I'd have a go."

"I tried to impress Lexa with my damp noodle," replied Peter with a grin, "but I couldn't get it to rise."

Auntie Sue didn't spot that he had made a rude joke, so she continued, "Perhaps there wasn't enough yeast, Peter."

"I don't think that was the problem," chuckled Uncle Peter.

"Thank you for that, Peter," said Mum, giving Uncle Peter a scolding look.

"It's the yeast I could do," chuckled Uncle Peter to himself while raising his glass of beer in cheers to my dad.

Grandpa tried to change the subject and lighten the mood again.

"So, Neil," he smiled. "How's school going?"

"Well, we've finished for summer now, Grandpa," I answered. "But I really enjoyed the end of term, and my report was pretty good. We learned all about ancient Greece in History."

"You should come and have a look at Nanna's chip pan," he quipped. "She hasn't changed the oil for years, so it's full of ancient grease." He laughed at his own joke. Nanna rolled her eyes. "And are you walking out with any nice girls now that you're nearly a teenager?"

It was my turn to blush. I answered carefully to avoid any follow-up questions about whether or not I had a crush on anyone. I didn't fancy dropping myself in it for liking Fleur. If Lemony got hold of that, I'd never hear the end of it.

"No, Grandpa," I replied. "But I might walk out on my own if I get any more embarrassing questions."

"You shouldn't be embarrassed about girls," he explained. "When I met your Nanna, she used to make my toes tingle… Nowadays, it's old age that does that."

Nanna was pulling on Grandpa's arm. I'd assumed that she was trying to stop him from saying anything else silly, but she was pointing at his plate.

"Don't eat that coleslaw, will you, love?" she said. "It'll give you Billy wind."

"I don't get Billy wind," scoffed Grandpa.

"You do, dear. You're just too deaf to hear it," clarified Nanna.

Everybody raised their glasses in my honour and there was a chorus of *Merry Neilmas* a strange Peel family tradition, before I cut into my pie. It smelled good, but I thought I saw something moving under the crust.

"There's a worm in my pie," I exclaimed.

"That's fat, dear," replied my mum, poking at the suspicious object with her knife.

"I know it's fat," I continued. "It's probably eaten most of the meat."

It turned out that Mum was right and the bit of gristle in my lunch was not a worm after all.

Nicolae was no less settled than before he went to the toilet. He was wandering around the table while eating a chip in each hand, and a constant snot stream flowed slowly between his nose and lip. Neither of his parents could be bothered to battle with him about sitting in the chair, but, thankfully, he only seemed to want to bother us and not the other restaurant guests. He noticed me following his circling of the table and approached me slowly with a look of malicious intent in his eyes.

"Ah, look," fawned Auntie Lexa. "Nicolae wants to give you a birthday kiss, Neil. How sweet. Give him your cheek."

"No way," I replied. "He's covered in snot and ketchup."

"Aw, Nicolae," cooed Mum, "have you got your mummy's cold?"

"Not Mummy's. It's mine," answered Nicolae before turning his attention back to me.

"A little bogey never hurt anyone," muttered Uncle Peter, pulling out his handkerchief and wiping Nicolae's snout.

"Try telling that to people who caught the Black Death," I answered, remembering my Year 6 history project. "You can't. Because they're all dead. Anyway. I don't want to kiss him because he always does something naughty."

Nevertheless, everybody was looking at us now. I lowered my face to Nicolae's level for him to kiss me so that I could get back to lunch. He leaned in but stuck his tongue out at the last moment and licked my cheek before running away shouting, "I licked him. I licked Neil's face!"

"I told you!" I exclaimed, but everybody laughed and cooed at Nicolae.

Hoping that he'd had his fun now, I wiped my cheek and got back to my steak and mushroom pie. Normality seemed to have resumed, and my attention was drawn to Lemony's conversation with my Auntie Sue, who seemed to be suggesting that Lemony should be going to confirmation classes by now. I was listening for the answer, although Lemony seemed to be preoccupied with something under the table; perhaps she was scratching her lower leg. A moment later I felt something touch my foot.

I looked opposite me to see if it was Grandpa, but he had fallen asleep at the table, his chin resting on his jowls. Another nudge to my foot, but there was too much tablecloth in the way for me to see who was kicking me or what was going on. Mum and Auntie Lexa to my sides were facing away from me, so it was unlikely to be them. I had time to look around the table and had just spotted that Nicolae was not in his chair again when there was a mighty tug at my foot, and my shoe was gone.

"Oh. My shoe's gone. He's got my shoe!" I exclaimed, but everyone else was too engrossed in their conversations to notice.

Deciding to go under the table and retrieve my footwear from the little thief, I slipped out of my seat and onto the floor. I scoped out my surroundings and immediately wished that Auntie Lexa had worn a longer skirt or could at least keep her legs together. Nicolae was at the far end of the table at Auntie Sue's feet, sitting cross-legged and grinning. He had my shoe in his lap. I crawled towards him slowly but stopped short when I realised that I'd planted my hand in a splodge of ketchup that had been camouflaged against the red carpet. Nicolae giggled and clapped his hands in amusement. There was a ketchup bottle at his side until Lemony's hand reached under the tablecloth and pulled it back up out of view. Two seconds later, Nicolae himself scuttled between Auntie Sue's and Mum's seats, out from under the table. I crawled the remaining distance to my shoe and slipped it on, realising my mistake only as the ketchup that Nicolae had obviously squirted into my shoe came oozing out over my ankle.

I must have let out a gasp of exasperation because Mum lifted a corner of the tablecloth and looked underneath.

"What on Earth are you doing under there, Neil?" she asked. "Stop playing around and come back to the table."

I contemplated my predicament for a moment. Behind

me I had Auntie Sue on one side and Lemony on the other. It was as if I were in that situation when you have an angel sitting on one shoulder and a devil on the other. I wasn't sure how Lemony and Nicolae had worked together to sabotage me on my birthday, but I was determined not to show them that they had beaten me. After all, these shoes had lasted me the whole school year and were too small for me to wear in September. This was probably the last time I would wear them anyway. I crawled out from under the table and took my seat calmly.

"Find any treasure while you were down there, Neil?" asked Uncle Peter, loudly, after noticing my return. "What have you been up to?"

"Just a small mishap with some tomato sauce, Uncle Peter," I answered, smiling casually. "Nothing to worry about."

Everyone went back to their conversations, but I noticed Nicolae, who must have scrambled back into his high chair, looking disappointed that I was not at all flustered by his naughtiness. I tried to glance surreptitiously over to Lemony but her expression was as bored as ever, and she wasn't paying any attention to me at all.

Nevertheless, I smiled to myself while chatting to various family members, using my peripheral vision to watch Nicolae becoming more and more irritated that he had not managed to bait me. I had to suffer discomfort for a short time before I could go to the bathrooms and scrape out as much of the sauce as possible with paper towels.

*

Once we'd all finished the meal, I asked if I could go and have a look at the fountain behind the restaurant. It was a big fountain surrounded by a wide, circular pool. Some people had thrown coins into it perhaps hoping it would bring them good luck. I was just thinking about the itch in my shoe from where the ketchup was beginning to dry when the restaurant door opened and Nicolae emerged, pulling Lemony behind him. He looked enthusiastic and malevolent at the same time. Who knew what these spawn of Satan had in mind? A distraction technique was what was needed here.

As they approached me, I took off my shoe and rolled down my sock, sitting on the fountain's surround and dangling my sauce-crusted foot into the cool water. I picked out a coin between my toes and brought it back up to retrieve it at the surface.

"Look, Nicolae," I called. "I've got a shiny coin for you."

I tossed it in the air and, miraculously, caught it again. How about that, Mr Ashley?

Nicolae broke free of Lemony, dropping two small objects to the ground in his excitement, and ran towards me as fast as he could. From around the far side of the pool, I tossed the coin over in his direction, but my co-ordination was less sure this time, and it dropped short, landing back in the pool again. In his eagerness, Nicolae toddled to the edge of the fountain and leant over to look for the coin in the water. However, his gusto was such that he overbalanced and fell head first into the pool and stayed upside down, his legs windmilling around wildly in the air.

My first reaction was to celebrate that the little devil had ended up the victim rather than me, but only a fraction of a second later I realised that Nicolae was not turning the right way up again. I met Lemony's eye across the fountain. She was closer to Nicolae than I was, but she was standing completely still and showing no emotion. Sure, I hated the little squirt, but this had suddenly become a life or death situation, and I could hardly let him drown.

Plunging my other leg into the cool water, I waded over as quickly as I could and yanked Nicolae out of the water by the back of his trousers. Thankfully, he gasped in air as

I dropped him onto the ground beside the fountain.

"NICOLAE!" yelled my Auntie Lexa from the restaurant door as she hurried towards us as fast as a pregnant person can. Her giant boobs bounced between her chin and her belly like pink jellies on a pogo stick. The rest of the family followed her out and circled around my sodden cousin.

"I drownded," whimpered Nicolae, burying his head in his mother's bosom.

"I saw everything," exclaimed Auntie Sue. "Neil was his saviour. He was a fisher of men, like our Lord Jesus himself raising Lazarus from beyond. He saved the poor child's life!"

"The birthday boy and a hero," said my dad, giving me the thumbs up.

"Nice one, Neil," added Uncle Peter, mussing my hair and patting me on the shoulder. His praise was a total surprise and the only time I can remember receiving a genuine, positive gesture from him.

Everybody congratulated me, apart from Lemony of course who pointed out that Nicolae would never have fallen in the water in the first place if I'd been able to throw properly.

*

An hour later, as we were driving back home with my wet trousers clinging to my legs, I looked across the back seat to my sister. I'd been thinking back to the moments before Nicolae fell into the fountain. He had let something drop as he ran towards me.

"Lemony, what did Nicolae have in his hands when you came out of the restaurant?" I asked.

"Oh that," she answered without turning her head to face me. A thin smile played around her lips. "He'd got two sachets of vinegar and was planning to squirt them in your eyes."

Charming!

CHAPTER 6

GATHERING FUNDS

After my double birthday celebration at the weekend, I still met up with the gang on most days over the next two weeks, but I had set aside one whole Monday to do odd jobs around the village. I figured that I'd need some spending money for the holiday, and the good people of Lower Piercing would probably be happy to part with their hard-earned cash in return for the quality services provided by Neil Peel esquire. In fact I'd already gathered about five pounds in change from the bottom of the fountain outside the restaurant at Itchington Fenny. It didn't bother me too much if other people's wishes came true or not, and I probably deserved far more than five pounds for saving a life.

I got up at around eight o'clock, pretty excited about how much money a young entrepreneur could make in one day. I'd got three jobs lined up already and was hopeful of finding a few more as the day progressed. First of all, Mum said that she'd give me some money for helping with the washing in the morning. Dad had said I could wash his car, and how hard could that be? The one job that I was less happy about was that Mrs Brady, the old lady who lived a few doors down from us, had said that I could take her dog for a walk this afternoon. This yappy terrier had practically savaged me a few weeks ago while I was in the middle of some athletic training. However, I put that to the back of my mind so that I could concentrate on my morning's tasks.

Bouncing down the stairs, confusion struck me as I heard the sound of the washing machine in operation. That was supposed to be my first job. Mum was sitting at the kitchen table with a cup of tea and a slice of toast reading the newspaper. The slice of toast wasn't reading the newspaper, Mum was while eating the toast. She looked almost ready to go to work.

"I thought I was doing the washing this morning, Mum," I said.

"Oh, morning, love," she replied. "Well, Lemony heard that you might be doing the laundry, and she was worried that you might have put it on too hot and shrunk her clothes or made the colours run, so she insisted that I do it. You can still hang it out though and fetch it in when it's dry; I'll pay you for that."

In a small way, I was offended, although not surprised, that Lemony didn't trust me, but also I had no idea that the washing machine had temperature settings, so she was probably right to be doubtful.

I had time to eat my breakfast and get dressed before the washing cycle finished, and then it was time for job number one. Mum helped me open the washing machine door, and I pulled out the laundry into the basket. Carrying it outside to our rotary clothes line, I remembered Mum's advice. The first rule when hanging out laundry: protect the gusset. The inside of underwear should face the centre of the dryer in case of *knickergred*. That way, if any visitors

44

were in the garden, there'd be no embarrassment. Knickergred was a word I'd invented as a small child for any kind of underwear stain. I assumed that that was the reason why occasionally knickers were tied in a knot in the laundry basket, although I struggled to see how anything could get clean in the wash if it was tied in a knot. I'm as guilty of knickergred as the next man. Unless the next man's my dad; I don't know why he insists on wearing white underwear. Anyway, knickergred may be unpleasant to think about, but it's even worse to display to neighbours.

One thing that did surprise me was that Mum seemed to have a knack for turning one leg or sleeve inside out in every one of her items of clothing. Only ever one on every blouse, pair of leggings or trousers. I started off pulling them back through but soon realised that she obviously preferred them that way, so I just pegged them out as they were.

This job took five minutes at the most, and I bounded back into the kitchen expectantly, waiting to see how much I would earn. Mum wasn't there anymore. Just as I was about to start looking for her, the phone rang, so I answered it.

"Have you been in an accident that wasn't your fault?" said a woman's voice on the other end. I wasn't sure that this call was for me.

"Who's speaking please?" I asked.

"I'm from Scutter and Minger insurance company, and I've been informed that you were involved in an accident that wasn't your fault."

I took a moment to reflect about this. Had I been in an accident?

"Well, I did poo my pants once in nursery school, but I can hardly blame anyone else."

Extreme knickergred.

The lady hung up, so I put the phone down too. Maybe that wasn't what she meant.

Mum and Dad came down the stairs together, fumbling with keys and putting on shoes.

"Here's two pounds for the washing, Neil," said Mum, passing me some coins. "Don't forget to take a key if you go out, and Lemony's upstairs if you need anything. There's ham and cheese in the fridge, so make yourself a sandwich at lunch time. I won't be back late. Bye, love!"

I'd spent most of the first week of the holidays at friends' houses playing Dungeons and Dragons or down at our tree by the river, so I hadn't really made use of the fact that Lemony was old enough to look after me if I was home alone while Mum and Dad worked. That arrangement had suited Lemony just fine, and I doubted I'd see her much today either. She'd probably be shut away in her room with her friend Ella Umber once she'd finally got up.

"And there'll be more money coming your way if you can make the car sparkle," added Dad, winking at me. "The stuff's all in the garage. See you later, champ."

Off they went to work; both were taking the bus since Dad was leaving the car for me to wash. I wasted no time in going straight out to fill a bucket with warm, soapy water; I didn't plan on getting cold hands for a mere five or perhaps even ten quid.

Carrying it out to the car wasn't easy since water is a lot heavier than I had expected. My plan was to start on top and work downwards, but, standing on tiptoes, I soon noticed that the roof of the car was fairly well covered in bird droppings. There was no way I wanted to get any of that on my hands, so I tried squeezing some water from the sponge over the closest deposit. Unfortunately, it seemed pretty crusty and attached to the car. When a problem arises, look for a solution. I toddled back to the garage to check if there was a cleaning product specifically for this purpose. Dad kept hundreds of tins, bottles and tubs of all sorts of paint, cleaning products and gardening essentials; there had to be something useful among them.

On one of the shelves, I found a tub that seemed perfect. At least I thought it would do the job; there were paint drippings all over the label, so I couldn't read it properly. It said '*Peel Away…. ain…. remover*'. I thought that could only be *stain* remover, so I picked it up and did my best to make out the instructions on the back. Again, there was paint splattered over most of the tub, but I saw that it did work on metal. I wanted to see how long to leave it on for. That, I could not find, but there were other key words I could see such as …*emulsion*… and …*takes off several layers*… I imagined that emulsion must be a French word; I had no idea what it meant. There was a black cross on an orange background and a hazardous warning, but I suppose the stuff has to be strong to get through the grime.

Using a stepladder, I applied the stain remover in generous circles around the droppings and then let it do its wonders while I put the ladder and Peel Away back in the garage; I'd come back to that later. Next, I set to work with the sponge and soapy water on the rest of the car. I must say that some of the muck was very attached, especially around the wheels and lower doors. Scrubbing really hard seemed to work in one small section, but that made my arm ache, and I could hardly be expected to keep that up all the way around the car. I realised that the dirt must have been caked on so thickly that it was now part of the car and would never be coming off. At least, not unless someone was prepared to give it a really thorough rub.

Once the whole car was all soapy, I took what was left in the bucket of dirty water and splashed it all over the bonnet and back window. The wet metal gleamed in the sunlight; I was pleased with my handiwork.

I was just racking my brain about something I had to remember when a voice distracted me.

"There are no idle hands in this house, are there, young Neil?"

I turned to be met by the broad smile of Mr Green, our

local vicar leaning over the handle bars of his bicycle. He looked the same as every vicar I have ever seen: bald on top with a bit of wild grey hair in a semicircle around the back of his head, glasses resting on the parson's nose, and a black shirt with the white collar. I pictured his wardrobe being entirely full of black shirts. We hadn't been to our local church much recently, but my auntie Sue always went along when she was staying with us, and the vicar knew everybody in Lower Piercing.

"Oh, hello, Mr Green," I said cheerily. "I'm just doing some jobs around the house and village to raise money for my holiday. It feels good to help."

"That's precisely the spirit, young Neil!" he replied. "Service is essential to cleanse the soul."

I wasn't sure what that meant, so I just smiled and nodded.

"In fact," continued Mr Green, "I've got a couple of jobs that need doing at church if you've got some time later on."

"Well," I pondered, "I'm taking Mrs Brady's dog for a walk at two o'clock, but I can be round straight after that."

"Splendid," he said, raising an arm in salute as he wheeled his bike around. "See you later, young Neil!"

Another job, although I struggled to see how a vicar could have so many jobs to give out when he only worked for one day in the week. Still, this was going very well. Two down and two to go! I hurriedly stashed the bucket and sponge back in the garage before heading in to make my sandwich for lunch. Anyway, there was a strange burning smell outdoors, a kind of chemical odour; I imagine somebody nearby must have been having a bonfire and burning rubber or something.

*

Still chewing the last of my ham and cheese sandwich, my brow furrowed as I toyed with the nagging sensation that there was something I'd forgotten. Just then another nagging sensation came into the kitchen: Lemony. She was in her yellow spaghetti-strapped pyjamas, her shoulder-length, brown hair messy from having just woken up. Loud, inappropriate music was blaring out from her bedroom. It was Durty Dreamz, of course: her favourite band.

"Still here?" she yawned, half looking at me. "Not playing out with *the lads* today?"

"Nope. Not today," I answered. "I'm doing some odd jobs to raise money for the holiday, remember?"

"Oh yes," she replied distractedly while reaching for some cereal from the cupboard. "However could I have forgotten?"

"Is there anything you need doing for a small fee?" I asked, immediately regretting my question.

Lemony put down the cereal box and turned to face me, one hand on her hip and the other on the kitchen worktop.

"Neil. If you ever leave Lower Piercing, then we'll have to advertise for a new village idiot, and I doubt anyone could do that job as well as you. The only thing I require of you is that you stay away from me and my room. I'm not paying you for that though. I'll just allow you to remain alive."

She smiled for a fraction of a second before turning back to her cereal bowl and closing the conversation. It wasn't worth replying.

*

The chemical smell outside the house was even stronger when I left that afternoon. Some idiot must have been must have been burning something really toxic. Thankfully, I only had to go round the corner to Mrs Brady's, and, as I got further away from our house, the smell began to disappear. Perhaps it was our neighbour on the other side, Dick Bush, who was having a bonfire: the fool.

*

I'd been uneasy about this dog walk since Mum told me that she'd arranged it with Mrs Brady. As I pushed open her garden gate, I could already hear the beast yapping away; he could smell my fear. The net curtains of Mrs Brady's lounge twitched, and I didn't even need to ring the bell before the door was opened for me. This lady was old. The phrase bent double didn't quite do her justice; she was bent quadruple with the middle of her back being higher than her head. She had to lean on a walking stick for support and twist her neck around to look at my face.

"Ah. There you are at last," she said, her dog growling at me suspiciously from behind the frosted glass of her living room door. "You're nearly a minute late. We thought you weren't coming, didn't we, Mr Woofles?"

I checked my watch; she was right. It was indeed thirty-five seconds past two o'clock. However, I was keen to stay on her good side since she would be paying me.

"Sorry about that, Mrs Brady," I replied. "It's Monday."

She cinched her mouth in repeatedly, moistening her lips while considering if that was a good enough excuse for my lateness. Eventually, she turned her body and invited me inside her house which smelled of a cross between the school urinals and my dad's old running shoes.

"Here's his lead," she muttered. "He likes to go down towards the park, but you have to go via Perineum Close because there's a special tree there where he likes to lift his leg. He hasn't done a dirt today either, so you'll need one of these," she said, thrusting a dog poo bag into my hands.

I'd forgotten that exercising a dog also meant dealing with its toilet needs. I hoped that the payment would be worth the unpleasantness. A lump came to my throat, and my heart started beating more quickly as Mrs Brady opened the door to reveal Mr Woofles; he may have been a tiny Jack Russell terrier, but he had a particularly loud bark. Mrs Brady gave him a little tap with her stick to quieten him.

"Be still, Mr Woofles, will you?" she commanded. "You have to be a good boy for Derek, or you'll have to go into the kennels until I get better. You don't like the kennels, do you, Mr Woofles?" Mr Woofles whimpered, understanding the reference.

"Who's Derek?" I asked.

"Who?" asked Mrs Brady, turning to give me a perplexed, blank look. "Well. Yes. That's right, isn't it, Mr Woofles. I'd be taking you myself, wouldn't I, if it weren't for having bandy legs these days. And I've got a corn on my bunion. Would you like to see my bunion, Derek?"

She started to hoist the bottom of her skirt so that I could see her misshapen foot through her tights.

"No, I wouldn't!" I answered sharply, grasping the lead in a sudden rush of courage and attaching it to Mr Woofles's collar. "We'd better get going. We'll see you shortly."

Mrs Brady barely had time to lower her skirt before I marched out of the front door. Mr Woofles momentarily forgot about savaging me, perhaps because I was no longer feeling nervous or perhaps in his excitement about going outside. I had, however, noted his reaction about going to the kennels and was holding that in reserve in case he rounded on me later.

Once we got beyond the garden gate, my bravado started to fade away, but the dog's eagerness hadn't. Mr Woofles was pulling me along his usual route, wagging his tail frantically from side to side. Sure enough, as soon as we got into Perineum Close, he hurried to one of the trees and cocked his leg, giving it a good watering. My relief that I didn't need to scoop up his business lasted another five metres before he squatted by the next tree and coiled out the most enormous, steaming dump. Seriously, it must have been about half the size of the actual dog. He seemed so proud of himself as he turned around to inspect his masterpiece, giving it a good sniff and then looking up at me for praise. Fishing the poo bag out of my pocket, I wondered if a single one would be big enough. I inverted the bag over my right hand and knelt down to tackle this gigantic chod when, all of a sudden, Mr Woofles darted off again. The lead was wrapped around my wrist and so he yanked me off balance. I had to put my left hand down to cushion my fall and planted it right in the middle of the turd. Warm faeces squelched between my fingers; I recoiled in disgust, dry-retching as the foul stench filled my nostrils. Mr Woofles turned around and cocked his head to the side as if to ask what I was doing, wrecking his freshly laid, curly cable.

Wiping it in the grass could only remove so much of the filth, and my effort to scoop the remainder into the poo bag was cursory at best; the area by the tree resembled an excretion explosion, as if a muddy garden sprinkler had been left on overnight. I hurried away from the scene of the misfortune, stooping to wipe my hand on the grass every few strides. After realising that this method would not be fully successful, I crouched to contemplate my dirty hand. As I was looking at the shameful sight, Mr Woofles padded up to me and began to lick my hand! Controlling my urge to vomit again did not mean withdrawing my hand; I allowed the slippery little, warm tongue to dart between my fingers, cleaning them better than I could have hoped under the circumstances. When we arrived at the park, it was a relief to see that it was mercifully free of anyone I recognised, and we only stayed long enough to make the walk last half an hour.

There was still quite a stench by the time we arrived back at Mrs Brady's house, but at least there were no visible stool stains. Mrs Brady invited me in again, remarking on how Mr Woofles and I seemed to have become good friends.

"Would you like a Jacob's, Derek? I've got mint and fruit Clubs," she offered.

"No, thank you," I answered, "but can I use your bathroom?"

As I finished washing my hands for the third time, I figured that I'd need to leave my hand in bleach for at least an hour before I was ready to tackle a 'Jacob's' or any other food for that matter.

Once I'd emerged from the bathroom, there was Mrs Brady with her purse open. Finally. The reward.

"Here you go, Derek," she said, pressing a fifty pence piece into my hand. "Is that about right?"

Fifty pence? That wasn't much even without taking into account a close encounter of the turd kind. Perhaps even Auntie Sue might have stretched to a pound.

"Well, thank you, Mrs Brady, but I think I deserve a bit more than that," I said. I wanted to be polite, but I hadn't done this for my health.

"I'm sorry, love. That's all I can spare. I haven't had me giro yet this month," she explained.

This wasn't a discussion that was worth pursuing. Oh well. At least I wasn't scared of Mr Woofles anymore.

*

"Young Neil!" exclaimed Mr Green upon my arrival at the church later that afternoon. I'd made a stop back at home to wash my hands a further five times before taking my bike and coming to see what the vicar had in line for me to do. He strode towards me with his hands clasped behind his back.

"I do hope you've a head for heights because there are some pretty stubborn cobwebs up there," he said, smiling as he gestured up to the church ceiling about fifty feet above us. "I have a large ladder in the back somewhere."

"Er. Mr Green. I…" I stammered, suddenly feeling

very alarmed.

"A joke, young Neil! A joke," he chortled. "No. The job I'd like you to do requires this and this," he explained, pulling out a cloth and a pot of silver polish from behind his back. "If you can polish the silverware we have in the vestry, that should be worth about ten pounds, I'd say. How does that sound?"

I replied that ten pounds sounded very reasonable, especially when he showed me to the vestry, and I realised that there wasn't an unmanageable amount to do.

Thus, I set to work cleaning plates and multiple lip marks from chalices. I thought to myself that, in communion, church-goers should be accepting the blood of Christ but not the backwash spittle of old Doreen from Gooch Street. These cups needed more of a hygienic, anti-bacterial clean than I was managing with mere silver polish, but that wasn't my brief.

Working in isolation can be quite relaxing, and it's fascinating what runs through your mind. I started to think about my holiday and how much I was looking forward to being there with my best friend, Stephen. From there, my train of thought went to the main threat to my fun – Lemony. That made me think of the song by Durty Dreamz she'd been listening to this morning. In fact she'd played it so much recently that I had, against my will, committed the chorus to memory. At least it was slightly more catchy than *Game, Set and Snatch*, her previous favourite.

I love your head and your toes
Flesh and bone!
Do you need all them clothes?
Flesh and bone!
Wanna mess up my sheets?
(Guttural subsonic guitar dive)
FLESH AND BONE!

"Finished yet, young Neil?" asked Mr Green from behind me, pulling me back to reality from my thoughts of what were probably some of the least appropriate lyrics to be considering in church.

Actually, I realised that I was shining up the very last chalice at that moment.

"Perfect timing, Mr Green," I replied. "Actually, I just realised that I'm shining up the very last chalice at the moment."

"Splendid!" he announced. "And don't they all look as good as new? I think ten pounds was the sum mentioned."

With that, he smiled as he reached into his wallet and took out a crisp ten-pound note, folded it in half and posted it into a collection box fixed onto the wall.

"The church roof fund is very grateful for your contribution, young Neil," he continued, raising his nose a little in superiority, defying me to question his decision. "As you said this morning, it feels good to help."

"But," I objected, "It feels much better to have helped and earned ten pounds at the same time! I need that money for my holiday. You decided for me. That's not fair."

"Fair? Oh, come, come, young Neil. Fair?" he responded. "Is it fair that the church roof is in poor condition? That Mrs Frew got wet through in the queue from the pew to the loo due to a leak? That the very church where your own parents were married is in danger of falling apart? You'll come to understand, young Neil, that many things in life don't seem fair to us at the time, but we understand the greater good at a later date." He put his hand on my shoulder and started leading me to the door. "The Lord giveth, and the Lord taketh away."

"He certainly tooketh away from me. Greater understanding isn't going to buy me an ice-cream or a souvenir from Majorca," I griped.

"Tish and pish, young Neil," he said. "Sacrifice is much nobler than such fleeting fancies."

"So, I'm not getting my ten pounds back then," I asked.

"No," he replied curtly, still smiling and ushering me into the doorway.

"Well in that case I suppose I have learnt something today," I said.

"Shall we pray together before you leave, young Neil?" he enquired.

"No," I replied curtly. "I don't think so."

"Toodle pip then, young Neil!" he exclaimed enthusiastically before encouraging me out of the church and closing the door behind me.

And that was that.

*

Pedalling back home, I pondered how I'd earned just two pounds fifty for my day's work so far. At least Dad was still yet to pay me for washing the car, so I was hoping for ten pounds there; this time it would be staying in my wallet rather than going towards the church roof. Rounding the final corner, I could see that my dad was already home. He was standing in the driveway scratching his head. As I got nearer, I could see that he looked perplexed and perhaps a little angry. I wanted to keep him cheerful to increase the chances of maximum pay-out.

"Hi, Dad!" I called merrily. "Did you get off work early today?"

"Not really, Neil," he answered. "Dick Bush from next door called me to say that there was a foul smell coming from our house. He said I should come back and investigate. I came home to find the car in this state. What happened, champ? Did someone vandalise it before you got round to washing it?"

"What do you mean?" I asked, confused. "I washed it this morning."

"But it's got dirty streaks all over it. In fact, it seems dirtier than it was before," he protested.

Perhaps throwing the dirty water back over the car to

rinse the soap off was a bit of an own goal. Nothing too serious, though.

"Then I looked at the roof and saw the state of it. What a mess!" continued Dad, exasperated. "State of that....state of that!"

He must have meant the bird poo.

"Oh yes," I said calmly. "I know what you mean. It had bird poo splatters all over it, so I covered it in stain remover from the garage. I forgot to wipe it off. Sorry about that. Shall I fetch a cloth now to finish the job?"

"Stain remover...?" asked Dad slowly. "What stain remover?"

"I'll show you," I answered, opening the garage door and fetching the pot that I'd used.

"Oh no!" said Dad, looking exasperated. "No. You didn't. That's not *stain* remover. It's industrial strength *paint* remover, you daft berk!"

Looking at the pot, I could see that only the letters *a, i,* and *n* were not covered by paint, so it could perhaps have said *paint* remover rather than *stain* remover. Oopsie. How bad could it be though?

I fetched the little stepladder and climbed up a few steps. Big oopsie. The top of the car was completely wrecked. It was true that there were no longer any bird droppings, but it was also true that there wasn't really any paint at all left on the roof. It had been stripped back to the bare metal.

"Sorry, Dad," I said.

Needless to say, I did not get paid for this job.

CHAPTER 7

AIRPORT CELEBRITY

The day had finally come. I was going on holiday! Excitement had beaten sleep for most of the night until exhaustion eventually overwhelmed me. I'd also had a stress nightmare about the flight, so the slumber that I had got was not as restful as it should have been. Nevertheless, I woke with a smile on my face, leapt enthusiastically out of bed, threw open the curtains to let in the sunshine, and checked my suitcase again. Washbag – check, swimming shorts – three pairs, anti PPI goggles – check, torch for late night card games– check, disposable camera – check, and secret chocolate stash in case Stephen and I stayed up late after the adults had gone to bed – check. I'd also brought half a roll of toilet paper because Vijay Jayasuriya in my class had told me that he had been on holiday to Spain, and the toilet paper in his hotel was like crusty tracing paper; I was taking no chances. My Marvel playing cards and Top Trumps, my sunglasses, and my Frank Beans book were in my rucksack ready for the flight. It was only two and a half hours on the plane anyway, so I had plenty to keep me occupied.

*

Dad was trying his best to look competent at fitting suitcases into the car boot, and I had been carrying them out into the driveway with him. Our car's roof had been resprayed and now looked better than before; I'd probably actually done us a favour by removing all of the old paint, but it was best not to bring that up.

"Yo, compadre!" came a familiar voice behind me down the road. I turned to see a car approaching. Ginger hair streamed behind Stephen's freckled face, his head sticking out of the window as the Princes' car approached. He had sunglasses on and was making a rock star hand gesture while biting his lower lip and banging his head in time to imaginary music.

They pulled up to the kerb and all got out to greet us. Mike was wearing a t-shirt with the slogan 'Stop staring at my tits' across the chest. He gave my dad a friendly man-hug before going to greet my mum who had heard their arrival and come out of the open front door with another bag. Diana Prince machine-gunned a laugh at nothing in particular as she got out of the car too. Stephen opened the back door and called over to me.

"Quickly! Into the time capsule! Step inside my office, amigo."

I climbed into the back seat next to him and we chatted excitedly about our adventures to come. I would be travelling with the Princes to the airport as well as staying with them in their apartment. It would make a nice change to think that I might not get a slap from my sister for crossing the centre line of the car's back seat.

Lemony's friend, Ella Umber arrived shortly afterwards with her dad. She was taller than Lemony with long, straight, dark hair. She already seemed to have a bit of a tan before we'd even left for our holiday.

"Hello, Ella," greeted my dad. "Looking forward to your holiday?"

Ella was just about to answer when Mum interrupted.

"Oh, don't ask silly questions, John. Of course she is. Take her case, and try to fit it in the boot."

It only took another ten minutes to arrange the suitcases in the two cars. Dad locked up the house, and I leaped into the back of the Princes' car. As we set off, Stephen wound down the window again and called out eagerly to the largely empty streets of Lower Piercing: "So long, suckers!"

The journey to the airport took just over an hour, during which Mike Prince made feeble jokes that made Diana laugh. Stephen and I chilled out in the back seat, occasionally groaning at his dad's efforts but tolerating them and still not losing any enthusiasm for the week ahead.

*

Tolerance, I soon discovered, was needed a great deal in airports too. It had been a long time since I had last been in one, and they were very busy places, full of some passengers bustling about in a hurry, others taking their time, and yet more standing about doing nothing, getting in the way. Everyone seemed to be pretending to be nice but really they were just pushing in to make sure they got where they were going before anyone else. While we were finding our bearings, a family walked past us, the father dragging his daughter along on one of those sit-on children's suitcases.

"I wonder if they do them in my size," asked Mike.

"They're not meant to take tonnes, Dad," replied Stephen before ducking away from his father's attempt at a blip across the back of the head.

We dragged our own suitcases to the check-in area and

joined the queue. Waiting around can be pretty boring, so I had an idea for how to liven up the next couple of hours. I explained it to Stephen.

"I play this game with Dad in the supermarket sometimes. We call it *Supermarket Celebrity*. You have to look at all of the people around you and decide if they look like anyone famous. If so, call it out. Fancy a game of *Airport Celebrity*?"

"Of course I do," he replied, "but be prepared to lose because I've already got a belter to start us off. Bill Gates is just further up the queue from us with his wife, old Madonna, and they've got Harry Potter for a son."

"Not bad for a beginner," I replied, trying but failing to stifle my laughter. I looked around for something to rival his offering. Too many normal people filled my vision until I spied a group of three student-types: jackpot.

"Over there. At your three o'clock," I said, motioning the direction with my eyes. "Where's Wally in the stripy top with Henry the eighth and, Zoinks, Scoob! The long-haired dude with the scruffy beard is Shaggy."

It was Stephen's turn to struggle in controlling his amusement, and we carried on through the whole queuing time. We'd both found about four versions of Queen Elizabeth but decided that not every bald man could be Dr Evil, before we finally arrived at the front of the queue. Just then I caught sight of the airline agent who would be checking us in: a particularly fat fellow whose face and shoulders seemed to have become one without the need for a neck between them.

"Bring me Solo and the Wookiee," I announced, just as Stephen spotted the Jabba the Hutt look-alike too. He burst out in a large guffaw, and we fought to remain straight-faced as Jabba called us forward.

We Peels went first, the Princes still waiting behind us.

"Name please," asked Jabba.

"Darth Vader," replied my dad, earnestly. "That's V-A-D-E-R. The asthma's cleared up, thank goodness."

"Only you could be so bold. Darth Vader? Now there's a name I've not heard in a long time," answered Jabba, smiling. Clearly he was a Star Wars fan too. "Real name?"

"John Peel," said Dad, grinning sheepishly and handing over our four passports as Mum elbowed him and told him to grow up.

*

We were a big group, but we were more streamlined without luggage, wiggling our way through the throng like a slippery eel. A quick check of the Departures board showed that we had plenty of time left before boarding so there was no need to hurry. Everybody had to walk through the duty-free shopping area where the advertising read: *Our prices are so low, it's practically shoplifting.* Lemony and Ella tried various perfumes while the adults examined the deals on alcohol. Stephen and I headed for the sweet section but were blocked by a rogue trolley left right in the middle of the aisle. A dark-haired man with a receding hairline and a pointed, goatee beard was kneeling down nearby looking at triangular prism shaped chocolates.

"Excuse me, sir," I said in a matter of fact way. "You've left your trolley right in the way. Nobody can get past."

"Well of all the impertinent things!" he sniped, standing up and pulling his trolley out of the way. "Young people are so rude these days."

"I wasn't the one blocking the aisle. All I did was make you aware of it, so…you're welcome," I replied before moving past to check the prices of the gummy jewellery further along.

"Shakespeare got his hose in a twist," whispered Stephen.

"Still, all's well that ends well," I joked, remembering the title of the play that Lemony had studied in English this year, and also aware that Stephen had scored another point in Airport Celebrity.

None of us actually bought anything in the duty free shops, so we reconvened under the Departures board to check our flight's gate number.

"Cringe! Flight delayed," exclaimed Dad.

"They've given the gate number but no idea of when we'll take off," added Mum.

"Still, best to get to the gate and bag eight seats all together," replied Dad.

We all agreed that this was a good idea except for Lemony who would have been perfectly happy to sit on a different plane from me if that was possible.

*

The gate was quite a long way from the centre of the airport, but, thankfully, there were plenty of those horizontal escalator thingies that made you feel as if you were walking really quickly. That is until you get stuck behind Albert Einstein standing still, smack bang in the middle of one.

"Beep beep. Excuse me," I said, our whole party snarled up behind him.

"Neil, please!" snapped Mum

"Oh, sorry," replied Einstein haughtily. "Am I in the way?"

"Yes," I replied. "It says 'please stand on the right' every twenty metres, but you're in the middle; no one can get past you."

Einstein reluctantly shuffled to the right, and we all passed him, the adults apologising as they went by. I didn't apologise. I'd helped that man not to annoy other passengers while speeding up our arrival at the departure gate; telling the truth had led to a win-win result.

Giant, steel birds (aeroplanes) were scattered across the runways visible from our gate. Some were being pushed backwards by what looked like tiny Lego vehicles before the marvel of modern aviation allowed them to lift off into the sky. Unfortunately, ours wouldn't be heading upwards for some time because the board at our departure gate was still showing that the flight was delayed.

Other passengers had arrived at the waiting area before us, taking up spaces willy-nilly. I tried to look for eight seats together, but the only row with anything close to that had a large, round-faced man with tiny ears sitting with five empty spaces either side of him. He had his head buried in a book, oblivious to the needs of others. Time for another Neil Peel intervention.

"Just off to ask Shrek to bunch up," I informed Stephen who grinned as he followed me. Sometimes my friends found my bluntness and honesty embarrassing, but I got the impression that he was finding it a pleasant distraction today, given that we could be waiting around for a couple of hours. I noticed my mum groan and roll her eyes as she spotted what I was doing.

"Excuse me, sir," I said politely. "We are a group of eight and we'd like to sit together. Do you mind moving up closer to either Will Smith on this side or Princess Leia on that side?"

Stephen chuckled, as did Princess Leia who had overheard and seemed to take my suggestion as a compliment. Fortunately, Shrek also found it quite amusing and was happy to move closer to the princess; perhaps he was hoping that she'd turn into an ogre after sunset.

Dad went to get everybody some drinks once we had all taken our seats. Stephen and I spent the next half an hour staring at the 'Delayed' sign, willing it to change while sipping our hot chocolates and spotting more celebrities.

"He's got a big beak, but that guy's definitely Winston Churchill," proposed Stephen.

"Jesus," I replied.

"What?" asked Stephen, confused as to why the man hurrying along past couldn't be Churchill.

"No," I said. "Over there. It's Jesus." I'd spied a man with long hair and a beard. Sure, he was wearing sunglasses too, but there was no mistaking the son of the Lord God.

We paused our game in order to do some reading, but I had barely pulled out my Frank Beans before realising that my hot chocolate had gone right through me, and I needed the toilet quite badly.

"Mum, I need the toilet quite badly," I whispered.

"Me too, actually," she whispered back. "We passed some loos a few gates back, I think."

"To the privy!" I announced quietly.

As usual there was quite a queue outside the ladies' toilet while I could get straight into the gents'. By the time I came out, Mum had still only moved a few spaces forward while I'd even found time to have a relaxing poo.

"You'd better wait here for me, love," said Mum. "Could you hold my bag for me, too? Don't worry. It's not really a ladies' bag."

"Mother," I reassured. "I'm a pussycat. I've held a handbag before."

Eventually, Mum shuffled forwards enough to pass through the toilet doors while I waited against the opposite wall. After a further couple of minutes, a tall, sinewy, snarling cleaning lady pushed her way out of the ladies' toilets and eyed me suspiciously. She had black hair with white streaks. Where was Stephen when I'd found the perfect Cruella de Vil?

"Can I help you, young man?" she coughed. "Where is your parent slash guardian?"

"My mum's having a wee, so no, unless you can speed her up, I don't think you can help me." I answered.

Cruella snorted and dragged her mop bucket away.

*

After Mum had eventually got out of the ladies' we went back to join the group, who were still waiting and watching the display in hope that a boarding time would be shown. However, everybody was holding a mini ice-cream, and Stephen had an extra one for me.

"Here you go, mate," he said, nodding in the direction of a little old man who was pushing a cart away from us. He was barely tall enough to see over the top of it and had sparse wispy hair behind his huge ears. "Yoda brought us all a free ice-cream because of the delay while you were in the loo. How cool is that?"

"About minus four degrees, I'd guess," I answered, smiling at his celebrity link and happily accepting my sweet treat. There was also some light background music playing to keep us all entertained during the postponement.

After yet another hour had ticked by, we were all getting pretty bored, and I was allowing my imagination to wander, wondering whether we'd ever be able to get on the plane. Although my egg mayonnaise sandwiches had been delicious, their distraction had only lasted a couple of minutes. Stephen was lying down more than reclining now, his hands in his pockets and his legs stretched out in front of him. New passengers had stopped coming past, so our game was running out of steam. However, Margaret Thatcher, who had been sitting at the end of the row opposite us, had now started doing some leg stretches and then lay down on the carpeted section of the floor to do some knee-raises.

"Why's she doing that?" I asked Dad.

"Well," he explained, "if you sit in the same position without moving for a long time, the blood can stop flowing to your legs properly, and you can get Deep Throat Veinitis. They say that doing exercises like that can stop circulation problems."

Not being a frequent flyer, this was news to me, but it sounded pretty serious, and I had certainly been sitting motionless for quite a while, almost going stir crazy because we'd been here for so long. It was time to move. There wasn't much room near us, so I stepped carefully over my fellow bored passengers' legs and belongings and headed towards the window. There was a hand rail there, and the view over the airfield made a change of scenery. I grasped the hand rail and squatted down before rising up again. Next came some upper body twists to the left then to the right followed by a few neck rolls. Stretching was a good idea; I was feeling much less stiff than before.

The music pumping from the speakers filled my ears and took over my concentration. My eyes were closed, and my head was nodding gently to the rhythm. In time with the beat, I swayed left and right, still holding on to the rail for balance. The music had got me, and I surprised myself by doing a few pelvis thrusts to the left and then to the right like a plump Michael Jackson. Although I was still facing the window, I could hear excitement growing behind me. I must have been starting something because people started clapping along with the beat and encouraging me.

"Go, Neil!" called Stephen. "You're winning at life."

I was clearly spreading joy as I jerked left and then right, pointing to the ceiling and then to the floor like those chaps in tracksuits do in music videos. The whooping of the other passengers encouraged me further into hip gyrations and side to side crab scuttles. I'm not sure exactly how loud the music was, but it seemed to fill my ears. I couldn't claim to be usually one for dancing, but this was living!

Bing Bong went the public-address system. *Would all passengers please make their way to the gate for Neil Peel's flight to Majorca where the most awesome dance spectacle ever is currently being performed?* Yes!

Even the baggage handlers down below on the tarmac were doing the conga and waving up to me. How they could hear the music was unimportant. A dot on the horizon grew bigger in my vision as my electric boogaloo continued. A few seconds later, I realised that it was my good friend Sam the eagle who had flown over, drawn by the musical commotion. He hovered on the other side of the glass, bobbing his head up and down and jerking his wings in time.

"Own it, Neil! You got yo' groove on," exclaimed Sam, doing a few loops. "Opulent moves. Everyone is loving this. You own everything!"

"Not too shabby yourself, my feathery friend," I replied, winking at him.

Sam started to rotate slowly before announcing, "I've got a surprise for you."

As he completed his rotation, I gasped in surprise to see that the beautiful Fleur Poucette was somehow stuck to his feathery back. She was the object of my affections at school, as gorgeous a creature as had ever walked the Earth. Her silver, glittery headband sparkled as did her black, sequinned dress. She bobbed her head along with Sam, her blond hair waving about in slow motion as she smiled at me. My cheeks flushed as she blew me a kiss and batted her eyelids. Confetti and streamers were falling from the ceiling around me.

"I still love you, Neil," Fleur said slowly, her eyes never leaving mine as she continued her graceful dance motions. "I always will."

"Neil, Neil!" chanted the voices of the other passengers behind me.

"I love you too!" I called to Fleur through the window.

"Neil!" The voices thinned down as Fleur and Sam were suddenly sucked backwards into a vortex in the middle of the sky. With one final spin, I slid to my knees, posing as if I'd just won the one hundred metre sprint in the Olympics.

"Neil!"

"Neil! You're embarrassing yourself" spat Stephen through gritted teeth. "What the hell are you doing?"

Reality slapped me in the face as my daydream faded away; I looked around the waiting area to see that a couple of hundred people were staring at me in stunned silence. A semi-circle had formed where other passengers had backed away from my gyrations, perhaps afraid of getting a clout from one of my spasmodic jerks. Nobody had in fact been dancing along or shouting encouragement at me at all. There was no confetti or streamers, and the music was barely audible really. Mum and Dad blinked as they looked; Dad's jaw was hanging open.

"I've never seen a few stretches turn into something like that before," continued Stephen. "You looked like Stevie Wonder getting electrocuted. Shouting 'I love you'? Where did you go, mate?"

"Does he need a doctor?" asked Margaret Thatcher as we passed her on the way back to our seats.

"Well that was interesting," muttered Lemony as I sat back down. "You've just given everyone a visual definition of 'moronically subnormal'. Try that again when we land, will you? That way they'll keep you in quarantine until the holiday is over."

I wasn't quite sure what to say; sitting around for so long must have got to me, and I'd drifted off somewhere.

"He was only doing some exercises," said Mum, coming to my defence. "Although, admittedly rather unique exercises."

"I was about to exercise too; exercise my right to complain, that is," said Mike Prince, standing up, "but it looks like we're finally boarding. Come on. Grab your stuff. Let's get in the queue."

It only took a few seconds for my embarrassment to fade before Stephen and I looked at each other and burst out laughing.

CHAPTER 8

THE FLIGHT

I'd thought that the next stage of simply getting on the plane would have been straightforward, but even that wasn't easy. We had got into a queue, but all of the first class and business class passengers had to get on first. They appeared as if from nowhere, like a trail of VIP ants having been relaxing in a special, comfortable lounge rather than waiting with the sweaty, restless masses.

A man of my dad's age and a much younger woman drew level with us in the prime boarding queue, their noses in the air discussing whether or not 'Barney had got the numbers right for the Q3 forecasts'. He was dressed in a smart suit and had slicked back hair. He appeared very confident, and the younger lady seemed to be nodding occasionally and smiling, pretending to understand him. She was very pretty, and I noticed how she blushed when the man occasionally put his hand on her arm or the small of her back as they moved forwards. They both smelled of expensive perfume, perhaps *eau de superiority,* and reminded me of Lemony's old Barbie and Ken dolls. I noticed a wedding ring on his finger while she did not have one. I wondered what 'business' they had to do in Majorca.

"Ken and Barbie," I whispered to Stephen.

"Frankly," said Ken, mockingly. "I'd be surprised if Barney has learnt to count beyond ten. You'd be much better than him in that role."

"Thanks," giggled Barbie.

"However," Ken continued, looking directly into her eyes and smiling, "I think you'd be much better staying in my team. There might be a promotion on the horizon where you could be in a position working directly under me."

"What a player," said Stephen under his breath. At least, he thought it was under his breath. Ken and Barbie, however, turned to face us.

"Excuse me, copper top?" said Ken, looking at Stephen. "Do you have something to say?"

"Err," stammered Stephen who looked suddenly nervous. Mike and Diana were looking through the bags for their passports, and my parents were helping, so nobody else noticed this potentially unpleasant scene.

"I think my colleague just meant to say that a married man shouldn't be saying things like that to someone he works with," I said, coming to Stephen's aid and now addressing Barbie. "He should probably be thinking of his wife and children during the whole trip, don't you agree?"

Barbie giggled nervously, looking to Ken for reassurance.

"Hmm," muttered Ken in response. "Enjoy your flight, back in economy class. We won't be thinking of you while we're sipping champagne in our first class seats with our personal air conditioning and extra leg room. Come on Barbara. It looks like we're boarding now."

"She really was Barbie," sniggered Stephen once they were out of earshot.

We inched our way slowly towards the front of the

queue and were just about to get to the desk when the attendant pulled the barrier belt across in front of us.

"One moment please," she said. "I have to help this gentleman get to his seat. Could you let him through?"

I looked around to see a man in a wheelchair carving his way through our group.

"Let him through to find a seat. Why? He's already sitting down," I answered.

However, she wasn't listening and moved past me to deal with the other passenger.

"Last one," said Stephen under his breath. "Stephen Hawking."

*

When almost every other passenger had boarded, it was finally our turn. Relief washed over me as we crossed over from the walkway into the plane; we'd been waiting so long that I'd begun to wonder if we'd ever actually be going on holiday at all. A funny feeling in my lower belly told me that I needed to break wind, so I looked around, noting with dismay that this area was still very crowded. All of our party was in front of me while Stephen and the few other remaining passengers were behind. There was no way I'd be able to squeeze one out without it being obviously me. This would have been no dilemma for Stephen who could summon up wind on demand and felt no shame at sharing it no matter how loud or smelly it might be.

A cheery hello from the camp steward, whose name badge declared him to be called Stewart Camp, welcomed us on board; he checked our passes and ushered us down the aisle. Luxurious seats with lots of leg room looked most inviting; one passenger already seemed to be asleep with his eye mask on, his hair trembling from the draught of his personal air conditioning unit in the seat in front. I soon realised that this was first class, and we were not going to find our places here. Just up ahead, I could see

Barbie and Ken clinking glasses of champagne in a toast. An idea came to me, and I nudged Stephen.

I waited for Mum to get a little ahead of me so that I had an escape route. My stomach muscles relaxed as we reached the two of them, and a low rumbler of a fart eased out of me. Sweet relief.

"Enjoy your air conditioning," I smiled, surging forward down the aisle, sure that my sandwiches followed by an exercise routine would have created a particularly noxious, eggy cloud.

Once out of harm's way, I turned to see Stephen linger for a fraction of a second with a concentrated look on his face. His arse suddenly barked like a sergeant major before he burst out laughing and scuttled onwards, 'the sarge' squeezing out more orders each time one of his legs moved forwards as he beef-walked to join me. Ken jolted, turned in his seat and spluttered, spilling champagne down the front of his expensive-looking shirt while Barbie pinched her nose in disgust.

*

Our seating plan had already been decided. Eight of us into three rows of three didn't quite go exactly, so Lemony and Ella volunteered to take their chances with a random extra traveller. Mike, Diana and Dad would be in front of them, and Mum, Stephen and I would be on the furthest row forwards, Mum by the window so that she could lean on it to sleep.

Stephen and I were almost at our seats when a big chungus of a man stood up and attempted to ram his luggage into the overhead storage. His belly was poking out from underneath a straining *Don't be jealous of my six-pack* t-shirt, bopping my dad on the head with each shove of his bag. He was also coughing deep, chesty hacks that needed swallowing back down.

"I hope he's not sitting near us," I whispered to

Stephen.

"What did you say?" asked Big Chungus, giving my dad momentary relief from having to lean into Mike to avoid being gut-barged in the face.

"I just said to my friend here that I hoped you weren't sitting near us," I repeated. "That sounds like a nasty cough, and I wouldn't want to catch your germs for my holiday."

Big Chungus muttered something to himself before taking his place which was mercifully on the opposite side of the aisle. However, the overhead storage above our seats was now full, so there was no room for my backpack.

"Excuse me," I called to Big Chungus. "You've put your bag in our storage locker. There's no room for my bag now. You should put your bag above your head."

"Hark at Billy Biggun over here," said Big Chungus, elbowing the lady next to him to get her attention. "What do you mean telling me what to do?"

"Well it is in our side, isn't it?" I replied. "And it's huge for a travel bag. It's no wonder you can't fit it in on your side."

To diffuse the situation, Mum squeezed past Stephen, took down her bag from the overhead storage and slipped it between her feet, leaving enough room for mine.

"There we go, love," said Mum. "Problem solved. I need my book anyway." She then leaned over to apologise to Big Chungus, but he had already closed his eyes, sunk his head into his jowls and was practically asleep.

My Frank Beans book was stuffed into the netted pocket by my knees, along with my Marvel playing cards, Top Trumps, and a bottle of water. Mum was contemplating her book, flipping it over from front cover to back.

"What are you reading?" I asked out of polite curiosity.

"Well, it's called The Constant Headache by Dinah Bordum," she answered, "but it's not as gripping as it sounds."

After ten more seconds had elapsed, she put the book away and opted for sleep.

*

My take-off nerves had been calmed by Stephen who had chatted away the whole time the plane had been taxiing slowly to the start of the runway and also while it built up speed. Once we were up in the air, Stephen continued his excited chatter about the girls we were likely to meet at the resort. He was convinced that they would have come from all over the world in search of a holiday romance. Neither of us had kissed a girl before, but Stephen was sure that this was the week to change all of that and that some lucky babe was about to meet her (Stephen) Prince Charming. While he was regaling me with tips about the washing machine tongue technique for snogging (apparently, Stephen had heard that it gets into every corner of the mouth), I was mainly thinking about Fleur Poucette. Excitement and fear were the two emotions that I felt in equal measure when I thought about kissing Fleur. It would surely be the most wonderful feeling in the world, but there was no going back to my current blissful state of longing once that door was opened.

My train of thought was broken by the appearance of a little child's eyes emerging above the seat in front of me. A little girl of about four years old giggled and then ducked back down out of view. After a few more seconds, she shot a shy glance between her seat and the one next before disappearing again once I'd met her eye, giggling as she did so. This would have seemed cute to my mum, but she was fast asleep leaning against the window. However, twelve-year-old boys aren't usually in a rush to get to know or play with little children, especially little girls, and I was no exception. I tried to keep my conversation with Stephen going so that she would get bored of me and stop this peek-a-boo game, but it's very hard not to glance at something that keeps slipping into your field of vision.

Eventually, the seatbelt light went out and the little girl in front slid out into the corridor. At first she just looked at Stephen and me timidly, but then she finally spoke.

"My t-shirt says Dreams Come True," she said, pulling the corners of her t-shirt down and beaming with pride at her reading ability. There was a pink unicorn leaping over a rainbow underneath the logo.

"I certainly hope not," I replied. "Last night I dreamt I was being eaten alive by a huge, ferocious monster, and the plane came down and crashed because of a gremlin eating the engines. Everybody on board died."

The little girl stared briefly into my eyes and blinked twice before bursting into tears and screaming, "Mummy!" She went back to her seat for a cuddle. Once her sobs had died down, we didn't see or hear from her again for the rest of the flight. Triumph.

A throb of excitement and happiness welled in my stomach as Stephen and I played knockout whist on our tray tables. The flight itself was not something I was used to, but I was enjoying it, and the weather forecast was looking excellent for the coming week. I was sure it was going to be the best holiday ever.

After an hour or so, my water bottle was looking quite empty, but my bladder felt full as a consequence.

"Excuse me," I said to Stephen, looking to move past him. "I'm feeling a urination sensation in my lower quadration."

"Understood," he replied, indicating the red toilet light. "Although, I think the fluid dynamics lab is currently occupied, so you may have to hesitate before you wizzinate. Also, I think it's Big Chungus who's in there, so be careful."

I glanced across the aisle to see that his seat was indeed empty.

"I'll be back," I said, imitating a line from a film I hadn't seen as I squeezed past Stephen.

Thankfully, there was nobody else waiting in the queue, so I could jig from one foot to the other knowing that I didn't have to wait long. A small child looked at me and asked his mother if 'that boy from the airport' was going to start dancing again.

There were some strange noises coming from inside the toilet cubicle, guttural throat clearing as well as relieved sighs. Eventually, the door opened, and Big Chungus emerged, chuckling to himself when he saw that I was the next one in the queue. I had to back away to let him pass, but once he'd gone by, I was hit full in the face by a wave of the filthiest stench I had ever had the bad luck to encounter. This made Stephen's best efforts at farting seem like a bed of roses. It was next level. A description of such poison is almost impossible, but I detected eye-watering notes of rotten fish, illness, old cheese, curry spices, out-of-date vegetables, rotten meat, armpit, dead animals, and good old-fashioned diarrhoea.

Turning my head backwards, I took a deep breath before fighting my way through this almost physical wall of devil's breath and into the toilet. I tried hard not to breathe, wishing that I'd drunk my water more slowly during the flight. Alas, I couldn't sustain it during the whole time I was peeing, and I had to draw in another lungful of that putrid foulness before I could finish and give my hands the most cursory wash ever. My slippery fingers fumbled with the lock as quickly as possible, desperate as I was to escape this rancid booth.

Stumbling out, I almost bumped into a lady who was waiting to use the toilet. I sucked in a gulp of clean air and smiled with relief just as she raised her hand up to pinch her nose, looking at me with disgust. A little girl next to her started to whimper and hid behind her mother.

"No. That wasn't me," I protested.

Other people nearby started paying attention to the scene.

"Don't worry, dear," said the lady to her daughter,

beckoning Stewart Camp over. "We'll ask the steward for some air freshener. Excuse me. This boy has made a bad smell in there. Do you have any…?"

"It wasn't me!" I interrupted indignantly. "It was Big Chungus over there. He was in before me, but I was too desperate to think of asking for air freshener. It's bad enough that some of that man's business is now in my lungs, but I will not have people thinking it was me."

With that, I stormed off, red in the face due to having to defend myself, although deep down I did not really care what anybody else thought. I was quite relieved to get back to my seat where Stephen was waiting to inform me that he was probably going to snag a girl who looked just like Black Widow on the Queen of Spades in my Marvel playing cards.

In no time at all, the captain was informing us that we were approaching our destination and that we all needed to return to our seats. I remembered advice to swallow regularly to ease pressure in my ears.

"Look at that view," said Mum, turning to me. "It's really taking my breath away."

"Not completely," I replied, sniffing close to her. "There must have been quite a bit of garlic in your lunch."

Mum raised her eyebrows before reaching for the mints in her handbag as the plane began its final descent.

CHAPTER 9

CHECKING IN, AND CHECKING OUT THE HOTEL

"Merci boocoo," said Mike Prince to the confused Spanish taxi driver who had picked us up from the airport in his minibus and dropped us off half an hour later at the Porto Yara Sofia in Cala Plata. We'd made it to our holiday resort, and I was so excited that I started doing mini-jumps onto and off the ten-inch concrete blocks where we'd stopped. How was that for parkour!

"It's hot as balls out here," observed Dad as he dragged suitcases towards the reception area, sweat patches appearing on his shirt in the armpit region. He was too encumbered to dodge an elbow to the ribs from Mum after his crude remark.

Pulling my case along with everybody else, I became distracted when I noticed a dark green lizard darting along the stone wall in my peripheral vision. It stopped as it met another lizard and climbed onto its back. I understood what was happening, but Mum had noticed that I had stopped and stood between me and the amorous reptiles.

"I see the local animals have their own version of *Follow the Leader* here too," she said in a matter-of-fact way before ushering me towards the automatic doors of the reception building.

Posters advertising various restaurants in and out of the resort flanked the reception desk while other boards announced the evening entertainment for the week.

A poster promoting *India's next drag superstar Trixie Patel with special guests Grotty De Boeuf and Butch Flaccidy* had captured the attention of Lemony and Ella who fussed around excitedly, noting timings and details of the show that Lemony was already hailing as the sure-fire highlight of the week.

As soon as Dad had got the keys, we all agreed that we should take our cases to the rooms, freshen up, and then head straight down to the pool to cool off after our flight.

The apartment I was sharing with Stephen and his parents had a central lounge with a little kitchen area. The two bedrooms were on opposite sides, and there was only one bathroom for us all to share. A quick visit to the toilet made me glad that I had listened to Vijay Jayasuriya about the local loo roll; how tracing paper was supposed to be comfortable or effective on your nether regions, I couldn't fathom. The roll I'd stashed in my case was going to give me quilted luxury throughout the week, as long as I didn't let anyone else know.

"Make sure you put your shorts on rather than your Speedos," instructed Mike to Stephen as I came out of the bathroom. "And do the strings up properly. Nobody wants to come face to face with little Nobby Nudger if you do some diving."

Stephen got changed in the bathroom while I excitedly got into my swimming shorts in our room. We had twin beds, and Stephen didn't mind if I had the one by the window. My eagerness mounted as I looked out over the pool, listening to the happy cries of children having fun.

When Stephen came out of the bathroom, he let out a loud "Wahey!" to accompany the six-pack abdominal muscles that he had drawn on his tummy with a felt-tip pen.

"You clown!" chuckled Mike, appearing from his room. He was short and stout, like the teapot of nursery rhyme fame; his considerable belly hung over his bright red shorts. Diana emerged a few moments later dressed in a light blue bikini with a light poncho-style top to cover her. She threw the sun-cream to Stephen. He was just finishing applying it when Mum, Dad, Lemony and Ella knocked at the door.

*

The Peel-Prince gang, adorned with sunglasses, hats, beach bags and towels strode out to the communal pool area. I'd like to think that we looked cool as if walking in slow-motion in some gangster film, but I imagine that the other guests who were staring at us were probably hoping that we wouldn't sit too close to them. It was mid-afternoon by now, and some people must have been having a late lunch or a siesta. My dad had been right; it was as hot as balls, and I could feel sweat building up on my forehead.

Mum spotted a group of unoccupied loungers, and we were soon settled in.

"Real men drink pink," suggested Dad to the other adults. "How about a bottle of *brosé* to start us off?"

I barely had time to hear their reply as I abandoned my sun lounger, donned my goggles and dive-bombed into the pool. Two seconds later, another splash to my left told me that Stephen had followed suit. Refreshing water seemed cold for a mere moment before I surfaced with a huge grin on my face. Stephen and I dossed about, splashing each other and dodging in and out of the other swimmers. Diving was allowed in the deeper end of the pool, so I suggested we have a go at some impressive plunging.

We had to wait until some space opened up in front of us, but I went for it as soon as a clear patch of water appeared in front of me. Unfortunately, when I hit the surface of the pool, my goggles slipped down my face, so that I could no longer see where I was under water. Reaching upwards, my clasping hands closed around soft flesh with a bullet-like hardness in my left palm and another between my right thumb and forefinger which reminded me of the knobs on Grandpa's old 'tranny' radio. Sucking in air, I realised that I was face to face with a late-middle-aged topless lady, whose bare breasts were in my hands!

"I'm so sorry!" I cried, releasing her chest lumps at once. "My goggles slipped off my eyes, and I couldn't see. I would never have done that on purpose, and I didn't think that your nipples would have been so low down anyway."

I was just wincing at whether or not I needed to add that last part when the lady smiled then laughed, saying something in a language that sounded as if it might be German. I think she was forgiving me, so I smiled, nodded, adjusted my goggles and swam away to where Stephen was looking for me from the other side of the pool.

"I thought I'd lost you, mate," he said before taking in a mouthful of water and then spitting it back out in an upwards jet. "Where did you go?"

"It was so embarrassing!" I whispered. "My goggles slipped down, and when I came back up, I had an old lady's bare boobs in my hands."

"You don't waste any time, do you?" replied Stephen, offering me a high five. "Second base within an hour of getting here. You know I was suggesting girls of under twenty years old when I talked about the foreign babes, but any boobs are *wicked*."

"Well, these certainly weren't *defying gravity*," I quipped.

Once Stephen's light-heartedness had calmed my

shame, we put our elbows on the poolside and surveyed the area.

"You know," said Stephen sagely. "You don't have to look too carefully to get some bazookas in focus. There is a serious amount of topless boobage on view."

Scanning the sunbathers around the pool, I quickly saw that he was right. There were all sorts of ladies who had decided to strip off: old ones and young ones, fat ones and thin ones, big boobs and small boobs. One particular lady's chest reminded me of a school trip that we had made to a local farm when I was still at Prince Albert Primary School. Several of us had had a go at milking a cow with particularly full udders that day.

Stephen followed the direction of my gaze.

"Oof. She's large and in charge," he guffawed.

I gave him a mock stern look. It wasn't nice to laugh at people for their size, and I was aware of my own little jelly belly when spending so much time without a t-shirt on.

Any kind of nudity usually makes me very shy, and I tend to leave the lounge if anything embarrassing comes on the television when Mum, Dad or Lemony are there. I know it's all natural and all that, but that doesn't mean that everyone wants to see it.

As we were resting and chatting in the water, I felt a few air bubbles tickle my side on their way upwards. The smell of chlorine was briefly overpowered by an odour that took me right back to driving past Rotherham on the M1 motorway when I was younger.

Stephen turned his head slowly to look at me.

"It is true," he said calmly, "that I have indeed guffed."

We both took this as our cue to head back to our loungers. To my surprise, nobody else seemed to have been in the water yet. Mum and Diana were lying back, sunbathing, mercifully with their bikini tops on, even if they had pulled the shoulder straps down; Lemony and Ella had moved their loungers a little further away from the others and were whispering together, looking across at the bar area; Dad and Mike seemed to have finished their 'brosé' and were now on good old-fashioned beer.

"How's it going, lads?" asked Dad, jovially. "Having a good time?"

"*Abs*olutely," answered Stephen, indicating his fake abs which had started to wash off from his time in the pool.

"Great, although I accidentally groped an old lady underwater," I added.

"You did what?" asked Mum sitting up suddenly.

"My goggles slipped when I dived in, and I couldn't see anything," I explained.

Diana machine-gunned out her laugh while Dad and Mike clinked their beers together.

"Disgusting little pervert," I heard from Lemony's lounger, although she hadn't turned around to be part of our conversation.

"Mind you," added Diana, looking around. "There are a lot of boobs out, it's true."

Once again, Dad and Mike clinked their glasses together and smiled.

"What do you think, Emma?" continued Diana. "Want to avoid the tan lines?"

My mum raised her eyebrows and shrugged as if to say 'why not'.

"NO! Don't even think about it." I cried, interrupting Mum before she could speak. "There's no need for that. It's uncomfortable enough with everybody I don't know doing it. Can't we at least stay decent over here? Don't you think you're too old for that anyway?"

"We're not in the grave yet, Neil," answered Mum, looking offended.

"We may have a couple of wrinkles, love," added Diana, "but mine are laughter lines. I wear my crow's feet like medals."

"What, round your neck?" I asked.

I noticed that Lemony had turned to face us. Her eyes were hidden by sunglasses, but she was reaching behind her back to where the clasp of her lemon-yellow bikini top would be. I also noticed out of the corner of my eye that Stephen's mouth had dropped open, and he had nearly fallen off his lounger to lean over, craning his neck to see what she was doing. It was no secret that he had always fancied my sister. Surely *she* wasn't going to go topless just to make me feel uncomfortable; she was still only fifteen! A look of horror must have flashed across my face.

Thankfully, she made an exaggerated scratching motion, smiled to Ella, and returned her hand back to her almost empty drink glass. Just as she finished her final sip, a young waiter dressed in the complex's uniform of a light blue polo shirt and beige shorts appeared between Lemony and Ella. He must have been about eighteen years old with shoulder-length blond dreadlocks, a scruffy little beard and piercing blue eyes.

"Hello ladies," he said to them with a confident smile. "I hope you are enjoying your holiday so far. My name is Stijve Tepels, and I can take care of you if you need something from the bar. Would you like me to move the shade for you?"

His accent was not English, but he spoke it very well. He pronounced 'so' as 'sho'; I thought he might have been Dutch. Ella blushed, but Lemony kept her composure, asking him to move the parasol a little and to fetch another orange juice and lemonade.

"And the *shame* for you?" asked Stijve, turning slowly to Ella.

"Yes. She'll have one too," replied Lemony before Ella could answer.

As Stijve walked back to the bar, the slightest smile appeared on Lemony's lips, and her head moved almost imperceptibly to follow him with her eyes from behind her shades.

*

"Who ordered the shredded beef cake? Take a look at that

fella, Emma!" whispered Diana, nudging my mum. I looked up from my Frank Beans book to see what she had noticed. There, on the bridge over the swimming pool, stood a youngish man in a very small pair of trunks. He was deeply tanned and was clearly proud of his gym-toned muscles. He wore shades and ran his hair through his sleek, black hair. It seemed that he had found a place to stand from where as many people as possible in the resort could see him.

My mum giggled and nudged Diana back. "Aah, some eye candy for the girls at last. Do you need some more sun cream on your back? Perhaps he'll do the honours for you."

"All right, you two. Calm down," scolded Dad. "I may have pulled a muscle just looking at him, but he's no jackpot you crackpots. Plus, look at his legs. He's a bit bandy."

"Oh, we are looking at his legs!" smiled Diana.

"Why would you want that when you've got this?" asked Mike, pointing to his own legs.

I couldn't help but look at Mike's legs, particularly his feet which I hadn't really noticed before. His toes were like the 'before' photo in a before and after fungal nail treatment advert, and they made me gag a bit. I wanted to wash my eyes after seeing them.

The hunky poser took a couple of slow steps across the bridge before he unceremoniously stubbed his toe on the railings and stooped down to deal with his injury.

"Ha ha!" chuckled Dad. "Are you sure he's not wearing those dark glasses because he's blind?"

"I don't care," retorted Diana, "if the blind man's buff!"

At this, she and my mum clinked their glasses together.

Adults can be so childish.

Lemony had clearly had enough of this high-brow conversation and stood up to walk away, dragging Ella with her. They wandered around the outside of the pool wearing sarongs over their bikinis. I noticed that they were walking casually but noticeably close to where Stijve Tepels, the pool waiter was working. After they had passed him, Ella looked back to see if he had spotted them and then turned to whisper to Lemony.

I shook my head and grabbed Stephen's arm dragging him back to the water again.

*

After we'd finished at the pool, we had dinner in one of the resort's restaurants, and then Stephen and I decided to head back up to the room instead of going to the bar to watch an old Greek man recreate the hits of someone called Demis Roussos. This didn't seem like something that would appeal to us or to Lemony for that matter, but she and Ella decided to stay down anyway, perhaps to see if that pool boy was still around.

We cycled through the Spanish language television channels until we found an American crime film. It was supposed to be suitable for the over 12s, but the leading lady didn't seem very fond of keeping her clothes on; the age rating system must have been much more permissive over here. At least her police partner had red hair, so that kept Stephen happy. We had been half watching the film but mainly playing Top Trumps for about an hour when there was a scratching at the door and some familiar giggling. The scratching continued until eventually the key was inserted properly, the door burst open, and in staggered Mike and Diana, supporting each other with their arms around each other's waists. My dad was close behind them.

"There he is! My boy!" slurred Dad. He stood there with his left leg planted in one place, but his right foot was stepping back and forth randomly before he staggered over to the sofa. However, his weight distribution was not as equal as usual, so he veered to the right at the last second and ended up behind us. He ruffled my hair and then got on his knees so that he could put his arms around our shoulders.

"You're good lads, you know. The best. I'm so proud of you, son!"

"Thanks, Dad," I answered, smiling with amusement at this drunken outpouring of his feelings. Stephen was recoiling a little from the thick smell of alcohol on Dad's breath. I was close enough to see that his eyes were quite bloodshot, and his focus was only half on me; his cheeks were flushed, and he was blinking very slowly.

"Well, would you look at that?" said Dad as he looked at the television to see the film's leading lady walk across the screen in a state of undress. He looked up to Mike with a daft smile on his face.

"I suppose I'd better go and see what Emma's up to," he announced before struggling to his feet, hugging Mike and Diana on the way to the door and bumping his shoulder heavily against the door frame. With a final "I love you, Neil", he was gone, slamming the door shut behind him.

Stephen made a gesture to me that we'd be better off finishing our evening in our room. Tipsy affection was funny for a while, but it was getting late, and we wanted to be on good form the next day even if there would be some sore heads among the adults.

Stephen used the bathroom first, and afterwards it was my turn to clean my teeth and then reflect on the day while sitting on the toilet with my secret toilet roll hidden under my shirt. Just as I was straining to 'drop the kids off at the pool', the door handle rattled noisily.

"Just a minute," I called, startled by the ferocity of the attempt to get into the bathroom. It had completely made me lose concentration; my poo would have to wait until the morning. There was a low grunt at the door followed by the shuffling away of feet.

I unlocked the door and stepped out, intending to tell

Mike that the bathroom was free. Not seeing him, I popped my head round into the kitchen area. There he was, swaying slightly by the sink, looking downwards with his back to me. He shook his left arm a little, adjusted the front of his boxer shorts and let out a satisfied exhalation of air.

"The bathroom's free, Mr Prince," I said helpfully.

"No need any more, Neil," he answered, smiling as he turned to show me a pint glass that was three quarters full of dark yellow liquid. He raised the glass in salute before pouring it down the sink. He then pulled out another pint glass that had been hidden from my view on the kitchen unit behind his belly. This one was completely full of similar dark yellow liquid. Again, he raised it in salute to me before chuckling as he poured it down the sink. Charming! I was pleased to see that there were no other filled receptacles, and I made a mental note to rewash any glasses that were offered to me in our apartment.

Mike raised a hand to say goodnight and shuffled away towards his bedroom. I couldn't help noticing that the front of his pale blue boxer shorts had a couple of dark blue patches that had joined together to form a sort of urinary map of Africa. I didn't imagine that he would be proud of this disgraceful scene in the morning…if he could remember any of it.

CHAPTER 10

LEMONY'S DREADLOCK HOLIDAY

It hadn't taken me long to fall asleep. I may have been excited, but travelling is tiring, as is being in the sun, as is swimming, as is staying up late. A combination of all of these activities had knocked me out almost as soon as my head had hit the pillow without even any time to chat with Stephen. It crossed my mind that all of our parents would have slept well with the cocktail of different drinks that they'd put away that evening.

The following morning, once an unfamiliar thin, bright rectangle of sunlight around the blind in our room had reminded me where we were, I sat up and looked across to see that Stephen still had his eyes closed. I decided to let him sleep on since he must also have been exhausted after yesterday. A cramp in my lower abdomen reminded me of my unfinished business of the night before; a slightly earlier start gave me the opportunity to claim the bathroom first. I'd take my clothes and get dressed in there too.

However, as I carefully closed the bedroom door, trying not to disturb Stephen, I was surprised to hear the sound of a kettle boiling. Astonishingly, Mike Prince was already up, whistling cheerily while making cups of tea. His hair was wet from the shower, and he seemed to be in a remarkably good mood.

"Morning, Neil!" he called. "Cup of tea?"

"No thanks, Mr Prince," I replied.

He glanced at the kitchen unit, picked up one of his pint glasses from the night before which he gave a cursory rinse before filling with water.

"How about some aqua?" he offered. "It's important to stay hydrated if you're going to be in the sun all day."

"No thanks," I replied. He clearly couldn't remember the end of last night at all. "I'm going to drink bottled water; I'm not sure I trust the local tap water."

Mike took a deep draught from the pint glass.

"Plus, you peed in that glass last night while I was in the bathroom."

He gagged and swallowed a little more before spitting the rest out. A quick sniff of the glass confirmed what I'd said.

"I thought it tasted a bit stale. Oh well. I'll give my teeth a good clean after breakfast," he chuckled. "That should do it."

I headed to the bathroom.

*

There was still some mist on the bathroom mirror following Mike's shower, so I opened the window as far as it would go. Turning back towards the toilet, I glanced in the shower and saw that the tray was much darker than I'd noticed yesterday. A closer inspection revealed that it was full of pubis hairs. Mike must have been very hairy, at least before his shower. Just then there was a knock at the door.

It was Stephen's mum.

"Are you okay in there, Neil? Have you got everything you need? Do you need a shampoo?"

"No thanks, Mrs Prince," I replied. "I need a real poo."

Five minutes later Diana knocked at the door again.

"Have you nearly done, love?" she asked. "That cup of tea has gone right through me, and I need to do my bikini line before we go to the pool today."

"Yes," I replied. "I'm dressed, and I think the smell has mostly gone."

*

"Ah! Breakfast. The most important of the morning meals," said Mike as we locked the door to our apartment and knocked on that of my parents, Lemony and Ella.

My mum opened the door with a smile, hugging me and asking how I'd slept. Lemony and Ella were just behind her, not showing any interest at all in how I'd managed the night away from them. I couldn't help but notice that Lemony seemed to have put on some make-up this morning. Not just to be alternative either; this was subtle make-up, and she looked very pretty, having clipped up her hair in an attractive fashion as well. She never usually made such an effort.

"Wow! You look nice, Lemony," I said genuinely. "You must really like that pool waiter."

She gave me an exaggerated sour smile before raising her middle finger in my direction as soon as Mum wasn't looking. Charming!

"Where's Dad?" I asked, noticing that he wasn't around.

"Oh, the demon ale got him!" answered Mum. "He's going to have a bit longer in bed and we can get him a few bits in a napkin as a takeaway breakfast. He says he should be right as rain with another hour's sleep."

Breakfast was served in the same dining room in which

we had eaten dinner the night before, and we were soon shown to our table for eight. As our order for hot drinks was being taken, I noticed Dad's empty chair and then looked around the room to observe my fellow diners. Pink and grey seemed to be the overriding colours in the guests' faces: pink for those who had stayed too long in the sun and grey for those who had had too much to drink the day before. Adults were supposed to be more intelligent and sensible than children, but that did not seem to be the case in this resort. There was no way I'd be drinking alcohol when I became an adult. That was for sure.

There was everything you could have wished for in the breakfast buffet and plenty more that you wouldn't have wished for in the continental section: pickled onions, gherkins and some of the stinkiest cheeses known to man. I had to check with Stephen that the smell was coming from the cheese and not him; he shrugged his shoulders innocently. We had a good week here, however, so I decided to try as many different options as possible.

"I am the egg man, I am the walrus!" came a loud chorus from across the room. "Goo goo ga joob!"

The singer of these nonsense words turned out to be a moustachioed chef who was entertaining a group of guests waiting for eggs to be cooked to order. He seemed a bit strange but strange in a good way, and I thought that an omelette would be a great idea. Mum and I met each other's eyes and nodded, smiling in silent agreement that we would both give it a try.

Stephen was drawn by the lure of a rotating toast machine and the fact that you could have as much as you liked.

"Unlimited toast!" he exclaimed. "This must be the best thing since…well, you know."

"How you like your eggs, pretty lady?" the chef asked my mum, raising his eyebrows flirtatiously. "Mario will take care of you."

Mum blushed while ordering two poached eggs.

"And you, boss?" he said, leaning on one hand and nodding at me.

I chose an omelette with ham and tomato. Mario made a big show of throwing eggs high above his head with his left hand while cracking another into a bowl with his right, amusing those of us in the queue. When he slid my omelette onto a plate in showman-like fashion and passed it to me, Mum thanked him.

"That was super, Mario. You're such an entertainer; why did you start cooking in the first place?"

"Because I was hungry," replied Mario without missing a beat. He then burst into laughter along with everybody who'd heard him. "Yes! Super Mario make a joke! See you again tomorrow morning, boss and you too, beautiful lady. I see no husband, so you let Mario take care of you again."

He winked at my mum, and she blushed again as we headed back to our table. I turned around, appalled at what I'd just heard, and I swear Mario was checking out Mum's bottom. My fondness for the chef had melted into disgust in an instant. That would be my last visit of the week to the egg counter.

*

After we'd finished eating, Mum asked me to take my paper napkin to the pastry section and get some plain bread for Dad. He probably wouldn't be feeling up to anything exciting, so I got a couple of rolls and wrapped them up.

"Hey, Joe, where you going with that bun in your hand?" called Mario from his grill which was much quieter now that the main breakfast rush had died down.

"Actually," I answered, getting things off my chest. "I'm taking some breakfast for my father, my mother's husband; they love each other, and he can throw and catch an egg too. He may have a hangover, but he's paid for an all-inclusive breakfast, so that's what he's going to get."

I felt much better after that and walked out as Mario held up his hands in mock surrender.

*

Mike Prince shook his head from left to right as he pulled himself up the pool steps later that morning. He sucked in his tummy and walked over to where we had set up camp. As soon as he felt less on public display, he breathed out, allowing his stomach to bulge out over his shorts. He bent forward to towel his legs dry, revealing a good deal of his hairy buttocks.

"I was feeling a bit better until you released the Kraken, Mike," said my dad from behind his dark glasses. He was reclining on a pool lounger and had managed some of the plain bread that I'd snaffled out of breakfast this morning.

"You're just jealous, John" replied Mike. "I've just done twenty breadths of that pool. Fit as you like, I am."

"What's a breadth?" I asked, looking at Dad's unfinished breakfast. "Is it a measure of bread?"

"Impressive," said Dad, ignoring my question and pointing back to his best friend's rear end. "But, and it's a big but, I cannot lie, why didn't you swim lengths?"

"Too many topless women at the far end of the pool," replied Mike, turning to wink at Dad and towelling his shoulders dry now. "I don't want Diana thinking I'm up to no good."

I groaned after looking up to realise that this was indeed true. You didn't need binoculars to see that there was a row of boobs facing us. I was still baffled about how uninhibited these ladies were. Maybe it was catching; one person had taken off her top, and the others had followed suit. I glanced over at Mum and Diana anxiously, but they had both fallen asleep on their loungers, bikini tops on; Mum's book, The Constant Headache, was still failing to keep her attention. Lemony and Ella had deserted the group without a word about half an hour previously.

Stephen noticed me looking at their empty loungers.

"I don't know why Lemony's chasing round after that Stijve Tepels guy," he said. "If it's a Stevie she wants, there's one right here."

"I have to give you points for trying, Stephen," I replied, "but it's never going to happen, so you might as well forget it."

"You may be right," he pondered, "so I'd better pay attention to the rest of the ladies. Where are all the girls our age? Everybody I can see seems to be over twenty years old."

"I was wondering where all the children were too," I added. "There was a club advertised in reception, but that was just for four to twelve year olds, so I don't think that would appeal to the likes of us."

"Too right," confirmed Stephen before muttering something under his breath.

"What was that, mate?" I asked.

"Pars-nips, Yorkshire pudding-nips and peppero-nips. Look at all of those nipples," stated Stephen, changing the subject rather dramatically and seemingly lost in thought. "I've been observing and making quite a study on this matter. The different shapes and sizes are quite fascinating really. Would you like to hear my findings?"

"Not in the slightest," I answered.

"Oh…okay then," continued Stephen, "but speaking of food, are you getting hungry yet? It's almost lunch time."

The workings of Stephen's mind never ceased to amaze me. I wasn't that hungry after my breakfast omelette, but a change of scenery would be nice, and it might at least have been a break from all of the bare chests.

We moseyed through the resort in search of something to feed Stephen, pausing briefly by one of the smaller pools. There, an animated young man was attempting to enthuse a group of young children in some pool-based ball game or other.

"Come on, Sugar Tots!" he cried, clapping his hands.

"Next one to score a goal is the winner!"

"So that's where all the children are," I noted. "I'm glad we're not involved with this club in any way. Can you imagine anything worse?"

Stephen nodded in agreement as we moved along. I couldn't say whether I noticed the *La Casita* sign or the lemon-yellow bikini first, but we were heading directly towards a snack shack where my sister was sitting on one of the bar stools. The pool waiter, Stijve Tepels, was leaning across, elbows on the bar, chatting to her casually with his chin resting in one hand. I stopped dead, grabbing Stephen's arm and letting him follow the direction of my gaze to find out the reason for our pause.

Stijve lowered his head, and Lemony reached over to stroke his dreadlocks. I couldn't hear their conversation or see the expression on Lemony's face, but he flashed her a broad smile as he raised his head back up.

For a moment, I was startled at seeing my sister flirting like this, but then I wondered why I should even be at all bothered. I didn't know if she'd had any boyfriends because she never bothered talking to me about her life and spent a lot of her weekends out of the house. She didn't seem to care about me, so why should I pay her any attention? Only after a few more seconds did I spot long, dark hair and realise that Ella was sitting on the next bar stool to Lemony, talking to another young waiter. Was I the only one around here who wasn't thinking about romance?

Stijve reached across and put his hand on Lemony's forearm, and that stirred something in me. I grabbed Stephen's elbow and ushered him forcefully in the direction of the bar. Just before we got there, Stijve let go of Lemony, picked up his tray and headed off. He grinned and winked at us as he passed by.

"Skinny Ribs and Chub," sneered Lemony as we approached. "What are you two doing here?"

"We wanted to know where all the other fine young

people were hanging out," replied Stephen.

"And we've come to get something to eat," I added.

"Don't you know that the waiters come over to you? You don't have to come and find them," she said condescendingly.

"Well why are you over here then?" I asked.

"Strange though it may seem, little brother," she snapped, "your sparkling company is hardly making my holiday memorable, so we came to talk to some people who've got more on their mind than breasts."

"Actually," I replied, "Judging by the wink he just gave me, I imagine that's exactly what the waiter has on his mind."

One-nil to me.

In my peripheral vision, I noticed Stijve making his way back to the bar. Lemony had noticed too, but she didn't lose her cool.

"Hmm. You still seem to be here when you need to be somewhere else."

"Come on, Neil," said Stephen nervously. "Let's just go."

"But you want something to eat," I protested. "She can't tell us what to do."

"We could look at this in one of two ways, but we're not going to," said Lemony drily. "You're buzzing off right now. Mummy and Daddy will order something for Stevie's tummy, so bye-bye."

At that, it was Stephen's turn to lead me away by the elbow just as Stijve arrived back at the bar. One-all. I knew that it was impossible to beat my sister, but I was happy to have won a small temporary victory over her.

Sure enough we got paninis delivered to our pool area for lunch and had fun in the sun all afternoon until it was time to head back up to the rooms to get ready for dinner. I realised that I'd enjoyed the afternoon more because Lemony had been nowhere to be seen since we'd left her at the *La Casita* bar.

"Could you go and fetch your sister, love?" Mum asked, folding a towel and gathering her things together into her beach bag.

"Do I have to?" I asked indignantly. "She basically told me to get lost earlier. It's so much better when we're not with her."

However, Mum gave me a pleading look, so I gestured to Stephen that we should head over in the direction of the bar.

As we approached the bar, I noticed Ella sitting on a bar stool talking to one of the waiters again, but there was no sign of Lemony's yellow bikini. I looked around but couldn't see Stijve either. Then, from behind the left-hand side of the bar, Stijve emerged, grinning while tucking in his light blue polo shirt and rearranging his dreadlocks as if he were getting dressed. To my horror, five seconds later, Lemony sauntered out from behind the right-hand side of the bar. She looked as cool as a cucumber and, without breaking step, gave the slightest of nods to Ella who stood up from the bar and scurried to join her. They headed towards us, Ella's head bent down to question my sister. However, Lemony didn't have time to answer her friend before she spotted us.

"Have you really got nothing better to do than spy on us?" asked Lemony sourly. She carried on walking past us without waiting to see if we would follow her.

"I'm only here because Mum asked me to fetch you to go and get ready for dinner," I said angrily. "We've had a great afternoon without you, and I'd gladly spend the whole day away from you again tomorrow if you need some more time behind the bar with Stijve."

Lemony stopped dead still looking ahead of her. Stephen looked from her to me and gulped. Ella did the same. I tensed up, thinking that I'd perhaps pushed her a bit too far. Slowly, she turned to face me.

"Well, Neil. I'm sure that we can find some way to make that happen," she said coolly before walking off with

Ella.

"That was tense, mate," whispered Stephen once the girls were a safe distance away.

"Well, if we have another Lemony-free day tomorrow then that will be fine with me."

I should have known better.

*

That evening, when we got back to our room from dinner, there was the usual resort information on the table in our lounge area. It gave bits of news about the weather forecast as well as activities happening in and around Cala Plata for the following day. However, there was also an envelope with a childish cartoon logo on the front and the word Sugar Tots printed in the top right-hand corner. Why did that seem familiar?

Mike Prince opened the letter and read a little of the letter before handing it to Stephen and me.

"It's for you two," he said.

Curiously, Stephen and I started to read.

Dear Neil Peel and Stephen Prince,

Thank you for signing up for the Sugar Tots Club tomorrow! Fun for everybody from ages 4 to 12 is guaranteed with our entertainers Felix Navidad and Ann Francisco. Meet at the Sugar Tots centre next to reception at 10 a.m. sharp tomorrow. It'll be the best day ever!

Best Wishes

The Sugar Tots team

p.s. €60 will be charged to your account, as agreed.

Stephen and I looked at each other puzzled. Indeed, neither Mike nor Diana could understand what was happening. Nevertheless, they were concerned about getting charged extra money, so we took the letter next door to see if Mum and Dad knew anything about it.

However, they looked as perplexed as we did when we showed them the letter.

"We haven't signed you up for any clubs, love," said Mum with a confused look on her face. "Perhaps you'd better call down to reception, John, to clear this up and make sure we don't get charged."

"I'm afraid there's no cancellation allowed," came Lemony's voice from behind me. She was leaning against the door frame of her room with a flat expression on her face. The corners of her mouth were ever so slightly upturned, showing only those who knew her best that she was very happy with herself.

"What do you mean, love?" asked Mum. "Do you know something about this?"

"Yes. He," she said, pointing at Stephen, "said that he wanted to be with the other young people, and Neil said that he wanted to be away from us for the whole day tomorrow."

"From you!" I roared. "Not everyone."

"So I seized the opportunity to grant your wishes and signed you up for the kiddies club for the day." Lemony almost burst out laughing, but she was too good to lose control.

"We don't want to go!" I shouted. "Mum. Tell her we aren't going!"

"What did you mean about no cancellation?" asked Dad.

"The club is already on the bill. When you two were added to the list, they had to get an extra member of staff for ratios, so there's no way to cancel. That person needs to be paid for coming in on an extra day. They were very clear about that."

"Is this true, Ella?" asked my mum, as Ella appeared at Lemony's shoulder.

"For God's sake," interrupted Lemony before Ella could answer. "I was doing everyone a favour. After what you said earlier, I thought you'd want a bit of independence. I knew you'd be missing your other friends. You know, the quiet one and the one with the glasses. Oh and the fat one who moved away."

I looked at my dad, exasperated.

"Well, we can't waste the money if it's already paid for, can we?" said Dad. "Lemony, you shouldn't have signed them up without asking first. That's sixty euros, but I suppose it is what it is."

"No it isn't!" I snapped. "She just wants us out of the way so that she can…"

"Well you shouldn't tell me your wishes then," said Lemony, cutting me off mid-sentence, "and I won't have to grant them for you. Anyway, this is tiring, so I'm off to bed. You should probably get some sleep too, Neil. You'll need lots of energy to keep up with all the other kiddies tomorrow. Goodnight all."

With that, she turned and closed the door with just enough time to wink at me.

"It might be good fun," said Mum, trying to sound optimistic.

"It had better be at that price," added Dad.

I knew what Dad was like with money; we weren't rich, and he hated any waste. Frustration mounted in me as it dawned on me that we would be going to the Sugar Tots club tomorrow regardless of any argument I could provide.

Stephen followed as I turned out of the door and went out onto the balcony. I gripped the hand rail tightly with both hands and let out a roar to release some stress. I was just about to tell Stephen that shouting had helped when I heard Lemony's mocking giggle through her open window.

"Come on, mate," whispered a sympathetic Stephen, putting his arm around my shoulders and guiding my back to our apartment. "Don't give her the satisfaction."

*

Once I'd calmed down and we'd got ready for bed,

Stephen and I were chatting before turning off the bedside lamps.

"It might not be that bad after all," he suggested. "At least you will be away from your sister for the whole day, and if we don't like what the club's activities, I'm sure we can do something else on our own. You never know. There might be some other cool kids there or even the pair of European babes that we've been looking for."

I thought of my friend Cameron's advice during my karting birthday party. The best way to make sure that Lemony didn't win (it had worked with Ottilie on that occasion) was to enjoy myself as much as possible tomorrow.

Even if it meant becoming a Sugar Tot for the day.

CHAPTER 11

SUGAR TOTS CLUB

I tried scowling at Lemony over breakfast, but it was hardly worth it; she wasn't looking at me at all as she sipped her grapefruit juice and slowly ate her toast while conducting her conversation with Ella in whispers. She wanted us out of the way for a day and had managed to achieve her goal. I didn't know what she had been up to with Stijve behind the bar or what she was planning for today, but it all made me rather uncomfortable. I was surely not being protective of her, but this was a discomfort that I hadn't felt before. Perhaps I'd thought that Lemony would go from being an annoying older sister to being married and out of my hair without there being anything in between. However, now was not the time to give any attention to her. As I swallowed the last of my third sausage of the morning, I decided that Stephen and I were going to make sure we had a great day.

*

"I'm so bored," said Stephen.

I was inclined to agree.

We had arrived at the Sugar Tots centre at ten o'clock sharp, as requested, but it seemed that half an hour had been allocated for all of the children to trickle in. There was a flip chart with all of our names on as well as our ages and nationalities as a sort of register, but once we'd ticked ourselves as present, there had just been milling around to do while the hosts, Ann Francisco and Felix Navidad fussed around the little ones, asking if anyone needed the toilet every few seconds. There were a lot of small people signed up for today; in fact we stood out like ballerinas at a rugby match, or perhaps rugby players at a ballet recital. It was unusual for me to feel tall for once since I'd just finished a year of being one of the youngest in my entire school.

"I might go and have another look at the list to check if there'll be anyone our age here," I said to Stephen.

He sat back in a little plastic chair and rocked backwards, waving his hand to let me know that he would stay there for a moment. I waded through a crowd of children, most of whom had either made friends very quickly with one another or had been coming to the club for a few days already. There were some peculiar names on the chart and all sorts of nationalities, European and from other parts of the world too. That made it even more surprising that they could all understand each other to be able to play together.

Mo Foe, aged 8 from Bahrain

Mohammed Dooley, aged 10 from Dubai

Shamone Eehi, aged 12 from Egypt

Dawn Corleone, aged 7 from Italy

Sam and Ella Eggs, both aged 6 from England

Archie Tekt, aged 5 from Germany

Adele Dazeem, aged 10 from Jordan

Dan Banner, aged 9 from USA
Conchita Best, aged 6 from Austria
Rusty Bizole, aged 7 from USA
Alan Keys, aged 4 from Ireland
Don Gloves, aged 7 from Canada
Mustan Sali, aged 10 from Turkey
Fernando Po, aged 7 from Portugal
Aubrey Jamm, aged 5 from the Netherlands
Lindy Hopper, aged 6 from USA
Gwynedd Paltrow, aged 8 from Wales
Neil Peel, aged 12 from England
Stephen Prince, aged 12 from England

There were twenty names on the board, and there seemed to be almost that many of us in the room already. However, I hadn't spotted the other twelve year old, the Egyptian Shamone Eehi, nor could I predict if this person was a boy or a girl because I'd never heard of that name before. Just as I was wondering if Shamone would have a really long chin like all of the pharaohs had when we'd studied Egyptians at my primary school, Prince Albert, back in Lower Piercing, the door opened and in walked a girl. Not just a girl. A very pretty girl. She was quite small for our age, but her rich, tawny coloured, smooth skin and long, wavy, jet-black hair with highlighted light brown streaks were the kind that I'd only really seen in Mum's magazines where the models were covered in make-up. This girl, however, had a natural beauty that made it hard to look away from her. She had to be Shamone Eehi.

After a moment, I snapped out of my trance, and, as she made her way in my direction to sign in on the flip chart, I turned to head back towards Stephen.

Just then, there was an enormous banging sound, and I noticed that Stephen had fallen off his chair. He had been balancing precariously in his boredom, but had lost in his attempt to challenge physics.

"I think I'm in love," he whispered to me as he picked himself up off the floor while running a hand through his mop of ginger hair, straightening his clothes, and attempting to appear as cool as possible. The noise of his chair toppling over had momentarily drawn everybody's attention to him, but children are quickly distracted by the next thing, and soon only Shamone Eehi was still looking in our direction. Her smile broadened as we looked back towards her, and the sun glinted off the braces on her teeth, dazzling us.

It was true to say that Shamone Eehi had a beautiful face and silky hair, but her looks meant very little to me compared with the effect they were clearly having on Stephen. While his jaw was struggling to close, and his complexion was reddening by the second, I could only see the image of angelic flawlessness that was Fleur Poucette. I got a funny feeling in the pit of my tummy whenever I thought about her. It was the same kind of feeling as when you drive over a humpback bridge without realising there's about to be a drop on the other side.

My train of thought was broken by several loud hand claps and the words "I am waiting, I am waiting, for you to sit down" being sung to the tune of Frère Jacques. It was Felix Navidad, one of the group leaders who had finally realised that he could not put off the day's activities any longer. He had close-cropped fair hair and a smile as fake as his tan. His colleague, Ann Francisco, a tall, tanned young woman with long dark hair, was rounding us all up to come and sit on the floor in a group in front of them. She had her hand raised in the well-recognised symbol asking for silence. It was all highly humiliating for us older ones, sitting cross-legged like we used to do at our first schools. In addition, my hamstrings were tighter than they used to be, so it was hard to find a comfortable position on the carpet. Most of the group was settled down while I was still fidgeting around from knees to bottom and back again. Silence finally fell just as I twisted around again, breaking wind as I did so before blushing and instantly regretting the third sausage in my particularly meaty breakfast. My face was now the same colour as Stephen's in his proximity to Shamone.

"Ooh, hello!" chuckled Felix Navidad light-heartedly. "Did somebody call my name? Come on. Own up. Who's Fartacus?"

Those who were sitting next to me knew exactly who was responsible; there was only one way to get out of this, and that was with humour.

"I'm Fartacus," I announced, standing up and adopting a strong pose.

Several children started to laugh apart from those who were close by; most of them were holding their noses.

"No. I'm Fartacus," said Stephen proudly, standing up next to me with his arms folded.

There were more giggles from the children before the American boy, Dan Banner, got up and also claimed to be Fartacus. Mohammed Dooley followed suit before the girls started joining in too. Pretty soon, all of us were standing, laughing and claiming to be Fartacus. Even Ann Francisco shouted that she was Fartacus and burst out laughing!

"Ooh! We've got a lively group in today, Ann!" exclaimed Felix Navidad. "Perhaps we'd best open a window though, just in case."

It took another few minutes to calm everybody down again before the plan for the day could be explained. It seemed that we would be spending most of the morning indoors with a choice of Lego, drawing, sand art or paper aeroplanes, before going on a treasure hunt around the resort. The afternoon would be based in and around the pool with some water polo and a pool disco. That didn't sound too bad.

In fact, the first part of the morning passed pretty pleasantly and uneventfully. Stephen and I had opted for Lego because that was one of his favourite hobbies. He could make anything with those little coloured bricks even without the instructions. I noticed that he only broke concentration every now and again to look over to the sand art area to see if Shamone Eehi was looking in his direction.

His skills were attracting the attention of several of the younger children after they'd spotted that he had turned a pile of light and dark blue bricks into a breaking wave with clear bricks making up the splashes. A mini figure was surfing through the middle of it. My own creation of an orange and white tiger was looking a bit feeble in comparison.

The little Irish boy, Alan Keys, had approached from the colouring table with a crayon in his fist. He was trying to lean past me to see Stephen's work better when he tripped over the back of my chair leg and crumpled to the floor. He got up slowly without the crayon in his hand. It was just at the same moment as I spotted the tip of something pink protruding from his nose that he burst into tears.

Felix Navidad was soon at his side encouraging the little lad to close his other nostril with a finger and blow out the obstacle with a *Fna! Fna!* He was terrified and reluctant at first, but after a few moments a couple of solid sniffs sent out three inches of sticky *hot magenta* crayon shooting onto the floor.

"Hey. I was looking for that," called Rusty Bizole, the American boy before scooping up the snotty crayon and wandering back to the drawing table with it in his mouth. I looked up from the aftermath of this mini-drama to notice that Stephen had been only half aware of what was going on. He was still staring over to where Shamone was helping one of the younger girls to make a sand creation.

"She's a goddess," whispered Stephen. "We'll have to see if she's got a friend for you."

"Hang on, Romeo," I answered. "You haven't even spoken to her yet."

Of course, I was hoping that she didn't have a friend for me unless she'd brought Fleur Poucette in her luggage.

*

The treasure hunt was to be done in groups, and Stephen and I were disappointed to be split up. Ann Francisco had clarified that the only fair way to run this activity was if the older ones took charge of a group each. I had Group 'A' comprising Mo Foe, Rusty Bizole, Gwynedd Paltrow and Conchita Best. There would be two girls in each group, again to split them up. My attempt to muster some team spirit was somewhat undermined by the fact that Rusty Bizole was ignoring my authority and trying to teach Mo Foe how to deal with bogeys (or boogers as he called them) using the 'Pick it, lick it, stick it, and flick it' method.

Felix Navidad explained that we all had a map and an answer sheet. For each of the eighteen numbers on the map, we would find a letter somewhere around the resort. You could answer the questions in any order and had to spell out a sentence before coming back to the club house by midday at the latest. The final application of sun cream was made, and then we were off! Four groups of children darted off in different directions.

Despite the baffled look of Conchita Best, my hopes were high for how we would tackle this challenge. Skirting between one of the apartment blocks and the pool brought us to a little children's play area that I hadn't explored yet. A quick check of the map told me that clue number seven was around here somewhere.

"Okay, team," I announced. "We're looking for clue number seven. Rusty! Moe! Conchita! Get off the swings. Gwynedd Paltrow! Get your head out of that box."

I noticed that she had found a cardboard box and put it on her head. After all, we weren't here to play; we were here to win.

"Actually, Neil Peel," she called, "I think this is where the answer is. It has a seven on the top and a letter 'O' inside."

"Oh. Well done, Gwynedd," I said, noting down the

letter on our sheet. The others reluctantly dismounted the swings.

Once we'd realised that the answers were inside boxes, we hurried around the resort collecting more pieces of the puzzle. Only after we'd found five of the answers did I realise that our team of five was down to four.

"Where is that little Mo Foe?" I called out.

A woman who was relaxing on a nearby sun lounger looked at me over the rim of her sunglasses and muttered something about disgusting language.

"Come on, guys," I encouraged our remaining team members. "We've got to do better. We've got to push ourselves and push each other too."

There was a scream as Rusty Bizole pushed little Conchita Best into the pool.

"That's not what I meant, Rusty!" I cried, pulling Conchita out of the water while Rusty stood grinning at us.

We retraced our steps, calling out Mo Foe's name as we went. Eventually, Gwynedd spotted him hanging on to a woman's leg like a limpet.

"Come on Mo," I urged. "We're in the middle of a treasure hunt. Leave that lady alone, and come and help us."

"No! I want to stay with my mummy!" yelled Mo, suddenly adopting a babyish voice and clinging even more tightly to his mother's leg. Her pained expression gave me the impression that she had been enjoying some time away from her son and did not anticipate seeing him back so soon.

"Look, Mo," she said soothingly. "The other children need your help, don't you?"

"Well, not really," I replied. "He hasn't been much help yet, and he doesn't seem to have any specific skills, but I doubt they'll let us win if we've lost a teammate. Perhaps you can come back to your mummy after we've got our prize."

"Yes," she continued. "Perhaps you can come back

later on this afternoon and tell me all about your day."

"Or I could bring him back after we've handed in our answers if you like," I said, being helpful.

Mrs Foe gritted her teeth and gave me a rather stern look and said, "Please don't trouble yourself. Later on will be just fine."

Eventually, we managed to prise him away from his mother (who immediately tried to hide behind a parasol) and drag him away to the beach burger shack which was the next stop on our map. In fact, we had to drag him round the whole remainder of the treasure hunt, crying most of the way.

One of the last clues seemed to be hidden at La Casita café bar according to the map. I wasn't really looking forward to collecting that one because I didn't fancy coming face to face with my sister's tonsil hockey match with Stijve. It was hard to be inconspicuous too when leading a group of small children around, one of whom was still snivelling.

Thankfully, there was a little path by the side of the hotel rooms which led to the bar without having to go past the pool, so I directed my team that way. Wet, mousy brown hair and yellow bikini shoulder straps were just visible over the top of the pool. At least Lemony was facing the other way and so would get no satisfaction from seeing me leading the other children…if we could be quiet.

"There's the box!" shouted Conchita Best, pointing over to the bar. Ella, who was bobbing in the water right next to Lemony, looked around and said something. Lemony did not look around but nodded almost imperceptibly. I swear she would have been smiling to herself.

We headed over to the box and Rusty Bizole was just doing the honours of looking inside it when Stijve Tepels, the waiter, stepped out of the side door to the bar with a tray of drinks in his hand. He smiled down at us with a look on his face that was either condescending or mocking. Either way there was something I definitely did not like about him. He winked at me.

"Remember, kiddies," he said jovially. "Sugar Tots Club rules!"

We filled in the letter on our sheet and realised that what Stijve had just said to us, *Sugar Tots Club rules*, was almost certainly the phrase that we had been trying to make. Was he giving us a clue or spoiling the game? As we hurried away, I saw him giving out drinks to a group of grinning young ladies. He winked at them too.

This guy really is a winker, I thought to myself.

With ten minutes to go, we found our final letter and ran back to the Club room to find that all of the other groups were already there.

"Where've you been, mate?" asked Stephen, walking over as soon as he saw us arrive.

"Getting the clues," I answered. "I thought we were doing quite well, but we seem to be the last ones here."

"Oh yes," he explained. "We've been back for ages. We found one clue but then got a bit bored. It seems that the pool waiter told Shamone's team what the answer was straight away, so I thought, 'if at first you don't succeed, ask someone else'. Plus, it was a great introduction to speak to her. We've been chatting for nearly half an hour, and she's so cool!"

At first, I was shocked into silence, so I just listened to him.

"We've got so much in common. She's Egyptian, so she loves cats; I love cats too, and I've even *got* a cat called…um…what's his name?"

"Monty," I answered.

"Yes. That's right. Monty. By the way, I'd better check with Mum and Dad that they remembered to ask someone to feed him while we're away. Shamone lives in a house made of bricks; I like *making* houses out of bricks. Lego bricks. She's got four older brothers and sisters, so she's the youngest in her family…"

"But you're an only child," I interrupted, not quite understanding this latest 'connection'.

"Exactly. So I'm the youngest in my family. But also, opposites attract. She's a girl; I'm a boy. She's dark; I'm pale. I'm tall; she's small. She's athletic; I've got no interest in sport at all. She smells sweet; last year, Basher Walker nicknamed me Corpse Breath. I like Dungeons and Dragons; she'd never heard of it and doesn't get it, even after I'd spent about twenty minutes explaining the rules to her. I'm sure I could get her to like it if I had another hour or so to explain all the little details of how our last campaign went. I think we're a match made in heaven."

*

Stephen spent the rest of lunchtime smiling and waving at Shamone while telling me more about how wonderful she was; she was looking after a little red-haired American girl called Lindy Hopper who seemed very attached to Shamone. Nodding along while half listening to him, my mind was more occupied with what I was supposed to do if Stephen wanted to spend the rest of the holiday with someone else. This was supposed to be the Lower Piercing boys' trip. I didn't want our Gruesome Twosome to become a Holiday Threesome, and there was no way I was going to be the spare gooseberry in the elevator.

A shrill whistle from Ann Francisco announced that we should all clear our lunch trays away before applying another layer of sun cream before our water polo game. The teams were already chosen, again based on splitting up the ages so that one team did not have all of the older children together. Some of the little ones were not playing because they weren't confident in the deeper water. Stephen nodded at little Lindy Hopper who was heading into the group that wouldn't be playing after Shamone had finished helping her with the sun cream.

"Apparently," said Stephen, nodding towards Lindy,

"she's a Mormon."

"Not a real one," I replied. "They don't exist. Anyway, it's pronounced *merman*, not *Mormon*, and she'd be a mermaid if she's a girl."

"No. It's a real thing," continued Stephen authoritatively. "A religious thing."

"Oh." I answered. "I wondered why she was heading to the non-swimming group."

Stephen was in the team with red hats while I was in the opposite team with blue hats. At least Shamone was in my team, so Stephen wouldn't abandon me to be with her. As soon as everybody's hat was securely on, excited children leapt into the water and splashed around enthusiastically. Stephen narrowed his eyes at me as we more mature players waited to enter the water.

"So, Mr Prince, do you expect me to lose?" I asked.

"No, Mr Peel, I expect you to die," replied Stephen jokingly.

Just as we were taking our places in the water, I heard Felix Navidad mention to Ann that they had forgotten to force everyone to go to the toilet after lunch.

"Oh, well. Never mind," she replied. "I'm sure they'll get out if they need to go."

For a children's entertainment host, she didn't seem to know children very well. Sure enough, many of the children stopped their splashing at intervals to have a quiet twenty seconds just bobbing still on their own with a contented look of relief on their faces. Had I swum closer, there would surely also have been a warmer patch in the water around them. As soon as that was over, they were back in action.

In terms of the actual match, the skill level wasn't particularly high. Dan Banner, one of the American boys who wore a bandana, even in the pool, was very energetic. He and I both went for the same loose ball which ended up bouncing out of the pool. Climbing out in pursuit, his Speedo trunks must have moved aside through all of his exertion, and as his backside was pointing in my direction, I realised that I was faced with the sack. Dad had used this expression once when he thought he might lose his job; I suppose either occasion would be unpleasant.

"One of your arancinis has popped out," called Felix Navidad before I had chance to say anything quietly. Dan rearranged his trunks and jumped back into the pool, thankfully finding the situation amusing rather than embarrassing.

I thought it was time for a change of pace and swam back towards our goal. Before I got there, Stephen took a long shot which bounced off our goalkeeper, Fernando Po's, head. He had been floating there with a look of deep concentration on his face, and he hadn't seemed to notice the ball heading in his direction at all. As I arrived next to him, his flushed cheeks returned to their regular tanned colour, and his smile returned as I suggested taking his place in goal.

I launched the ball out to Mustan Sali on our left wing and then held on to the side to watch the action, ducking my head underwater to pass the time while my team was attacking. With one such head dip, I noticed a small dark shape on the bottom of the pool. Securing my goggles and taking a deeper breath, I descended again for a closer inspection. Only when very close up and about to reach out to collect the object, did I realise that I was about to scoop up a turd. The look of intense concentration on Fernando Po's face now made sense. I called Felix Navidad over, trying to be sensitive to the poor little boy's predicament.

"I think you should have remembered to make everybody go to the toilet after lunch. I'm afraid there's been a mishap, and now there's a poo at the bottom of the pool."

Felix's smile faded and a look of disgust replaced it. For a moment, I felt that his disgust might have been towards me. Perhaps my explanation hadn't been clear enough. He called over one of the pool attendants who arrived with a net on a stick and a grumpy look on his face. I pointed to where the business card had been left.

"Why you sheet in the pool?" asked the attendant as he dipped his net into the water.

Before I had time to answer, Felix was blowing his shrill whistle and ushering everybody to abandon the game and move to the shallow end of the pool.

"Neil's done an accident, everybody. Game over, I'm afraid," he yelled.

What?!

"It wasn't me," I roared, any hopes of being discreet for the Portuguese boy flying out of the window. "It was that, that…Portugal boy… that Portugeezer," I announced, temporarily forgetting his name. "It was Fernando Po!" I shouted, suddenly remembering his name and pointing over to him. This was just like being accused of making the bad smell in the aeroplane toilet. Why did I keep getting the blame? I really had bad luck when it came to being in the wrong smelly place at the wrong smelly time.

Fortunately, most of the children were too young to be bothered, perhaps even finding any bodily function just hilarious. However, I was concerned as to what Shamone would think of me; I knew Stephen would believe me, but I hadn't even spoken to her yet.

At that moment, Ann Francisco started the music and lights at the shallow end of the pool, and the disco had begun. It was slightly earlier than planned due to the scatological interruption, but everybody was soon bopping around and singing along with songs that they all knew, no matter what their country of origin while the pool attendant fished around with his net in the deep end.

Felix was leading the dancing from the poolside, generally pointing to the floor or the sky or covering his crotch with his palm. The Sugar Tots were in full flow, and Stephen and I were not missing out. The *crab scuttle* that I thought I'd perfected at the airport was brought back, much to Stephen's amusement. He invented a move called the *giant squid roll* which involved spinning around with your arms flailing about. I thought some underwater handstands would be a cool thing to try and so found a bit of space and went for it. I was quite good a keeping my balance, and I thought I'd been upright for a good twenty seconds. Finally, I broke my pose and surfaced, ready for a high-five from Stephen. However, I couldn't see him anymore. Not, that is, until his giant squid roll surfaced across the other side of the pool. He hadn't been watching my impressive handstand at all; he'd moved next to Shamone and was laughing with her. Again, I was temporarily unaware of how to handle the situation. Should I go over and mess around with them or give them some space? The loud music would have meant that I couldn't really have introduced myself properly anyway, so I swam slowly over to the side of the pool and observed everybody. After a few minutes, I began to feel quite sorry for myself. The younger children occasionally looked up at me from their dancing with a smile that invited me to jump back in and have fun, but it wouldn't be fun for me without my best friend there. I was having trouble understanding how Stephen could be enjoying his time with Shamone more than with me.

Song after song went by, and still Stephen didn't seem to notice that he'd effectively ditched me.

"Keep dancing, Sugar Tots!" yelled Ann Francisco into the microphone. "We've got half an hour left."

"When will it end?" I said to myself but also out loud while throwing my head back.

"In half an hour," answered a familiar voice next to me.

Stephen's ginger hair had emerged from the water next to me, a beaming smile on his face. I checked to see that he was alone.

"Sorry, mate," he started. "Shamone called me over, so I started dancing with her and lost track of time. Was I gone long?"

"Yes," I replied. "A really long time."

"You should have come over," he said, jovially. "I need to introduce you anyway."

"I didn't want to get in your way, and I don't usually know what to say to girls anyway," I explained.

"You needn't have worried," continued Stephen. "I tried to carry on explaining about Dungeons and Dragons to her – I could have used your help there, but she said the music was too loud to hear properly."

"Mate, do you think she wants to hear about Dungeons and Dragons?" I asked.

Stephen looked puzzled.

"Hmm. I hadn't thought of that," he admitted. "Anyway, she had to go early, and she's off exploring the island tomorrow, so why don't I make it up to you, and we can do some cliff diving tomorrow, just me and you?"

Stephen explained what was involved and said that he and his dad had done it many times before. I thought this sounded like a really very good idea.

The disco eventually finished, so we said goodbye to the little ones as well as Ann Francisco and Felix Navidad.

"Will you be back to join us again tomorrow?" asked Felix.

"No," I replied. "But it wasn't half as bad as I'd expected it to be."

We gathered our things before heading back to join our families by the main pool. It wasn't hard to see where they were; in fact, raised voices meant we could hear where they were before seeing them. It looked as if Dad was being told off by Lemony.

"…and you can mind your own business. I don't want to talk about it anymore."

Ella was just about to say something when Lemony cut her off.

"Come on, Ella," she commanded. "Let's go back to the apartment. Key, please, mother?"

She held her hand out expectantly, and Mum duly fished the key out of her bag and handed it over. Mum also seemed to be looking sourly at Dad, and I could also notice that Diana Prince seemed to be scowling at Mike.

"One day spent away from you all, and the Peel-Prince ship is sinking," I announced.

"Oh, the lads are back," greeted Mike, seemingly glad of some distraction from the bad atmosphere.

"How was the club?" asked Mum, forcing a smile.

"They all loved us," replied Stephen.

"But we're not going back," I added just to be clear.

Once everything had been collected and stuffed into beach bags, we all trudged off back to the apartments. I hung back to ask Dad what all the beef was about.

"I'd gone to fetch Lemony from the pool bar to come and get ready for dinner, but I didn't expect to have to prise her away from the waiter. I only asked if she knew what she was doing," he explained.

"But why is Mum being grumpy about that?" I asked, understanding Lemony's anger but not Mum's.

"Oh, that's something else," he whispered, trying not to be heard. "It's about tomorrow. Take my advice: don't get married and never have children. All I want to do is relax with my friend on holiday. I don't think that's too much to ask."

Having expected to side with my mum, I found that this was not the case at all, and my dad's words struck a chord. After all, I wanted to spend my holiday time with my best friend too, and a girl was getting in the way. Since the 'girl' in Dad's situation was my mother, I had to re-evaluate my thoughts.

*

Dinner that evening was quite uncomfortable with sour looks being passed between most of the adults and Lemony. It seemed that despite not wanting to go to the

Sugar Tots club, Stephen and I were the ones who'd ended the day the happiest.

As I lay in bed that night, listening to Stephen's gentle snuffles, I made the mature decision that, after tomorrow, I was going to have to allow him some time with Shamone without getting upset about it. Surely that was the least I could do. After all, everybody else needed a little Neil Peel sparkle to avoid falling out with each other.

CHAPTER 12

THE MISSING KEY

It was clear why Lemony had wanted us out of the way yesterday, but Stephen and I wouldn't be so easy to fool today. Having said that, I had no desire to see her smooching with Stijve Tepels, so Stephen and I had come up with plan B.

"We're going out to explore the island this morning," announced Mum as we sat around the breakfast table finishing off our buffet breakfast. "Get a bit of culture. There's a minibus heading out in an hour to the Sotomayor monastery and then on to Puerto del Carmen port where we can have lunch. The guide book says it's beautiful."

My dad and Mike glanced at each other and then looked down at the table. They looked like naughty schoolboys and had both clearly been persuaded into this trip against their will. That explained the unpleasant atmosphere of yesterday evening. I, however, was not going to give in so easily.

"Well, I hope you enjoy that, but we're not coming with you."

"But darling," said Mum, putting her hand on mine, "you can't stay here on your own. You're only twelve years old."

"That's true," I continued, "but you have to understand that young people just don't like that sort of thing. We'd get bored before we'd even got on the bus, and we'd probably ruin the whole trip for you. Anyway, I'm not on my own. Stephen's here too."

My dad's face told me that young people weren't the only ones who didn't enjoy such visits, but he had been beaten into submission and realised that he had no alternative but to go along.

"Have Mike and I got time for a quick drink in the bar before we set off, love?" asked Dad.

"No, you haven't!" snapped Mum.

"I only meant a quick one since I'm not driving," replied Dad softly.

"You are. You're driving me mad," answered Mum.

Dad stayed quiet.

"The boys could stay by the pool if that'd make you feel better, Emma," suggested Diana who was never worried about Stephen.

"I hope you don't expect us to come along too," interjected Lemony, "because that's not happening, is it Ella?"

Ella opened her mouth to speak before Mum interrupted her.

"I suppose if the girls are staying to keep an eye on you then that should be okay."

"But we wanted to go to the cape today to do some cliff jumping," protested Stephen.

"Isn't that a bit dangerous?" asked Mum, looking nervous.

"We've done it loads of times," said Mike confidently.

"Mind you, it does scare something out of me because I usually leave a motion in the ocean after I've jumped."

"It's only five minutes away from the resort, Emma," said Diana. "It's a path that leads directly from here, and it's really easy to get to."

"Well, all right," conceded Mum. "As long as you're careful."

After breakfast we went back to the apartment where Stephen and I were ready for the day in no time. Adults seemed to take a bit longer, especially as Mike always needed time for a post-breakfast poo, so we had time for a couple of games of Knock-Out Whist with my Marvel playing cards. Stephen hadn't even mentioned Shamone this morning, and I had a feeling that this was a good omen. Eventually, Mike and Diana came out of their room looking ready for their day.

"Have you got your sun cream on yet?" Diana asked Stephen.

"No. Not yet," he replied while clearing up the cards.

I went to fetch his factor 50 and my factor 30 from the bathroom, and we covered ourselves. Noticing his mum's wide-brimmed sun hat, Stephen put on his red tuna cap. Initially, it was called a tuna cap because it had a tuna fish as a surfing logo on it, but that had faded away long ago. However, there must have been something in the dye because it now reeked of a mixture of stale urine and rotten meat. Stephen refused to wear anything else on his head out of loyalty to the cap.

"We'll be out for lunch," said Mike, locking the apartment door behind us, "so you'd better look after the key. You'll probably have to come back and get changed after your cliff jumping. Don't lose it though because we've only got one."

"No problem, Dad," said Stephen, pocketing the key. We had a bag between us of towels, water, and extra sun cream. I'd brought my goggles too, just in case, although Stephen said you couldn't really jump in with them on as they'd probably fall off on impact with the water. I was unlikely to come hand to breast with any more German ladies, but it was best to be prepared.

We knocked on Mum and Dad's door, and they too were ready. Mum fussed around me somewhat, asking about sun cream and reminding me to be careful. She then checked whether Lemony and Ella had everything they needed.

"Yes. You already asked," snapped Lemony. "I've got the key, and we've got everything else in the bag."

"How about you, Ella?" asked Mum, but before Ella could answer, Mike interrupted.

"And if you boys break both of your legs, don't come running to us."

There were final goodbyes before the parents headed down to reception to wait for their minibus. I was about to say something to Lemony about lunch, but she had already grabbed Ella's arm and was leading her towards the pool area, probably in search of Stijve.

"Right then," said Stephen, straightening the brim of his tuna cap. "Let's roll."

It was another beautiful day of blue skies and full sunshine, and it really was only a short walk to the cape. There were a couple of other people already at the jumping spot, so we dumped our bag and looked out to see how far the drop was. Eighty metres was my first guess but Stephen informed me that it was not even nine. We watched as a young boy of about nine years old took a run-up and leapt out, flailing his arms and singing *Old MacDonald had a Farm* as quickly as possible. He managed to get to the first *E-I* before hitting the water, resurfacing and looking up to his laughing father for approval. The little chap climbed out of the water and clambered up the path that was worn into the rocks. He was half way back up to the top when his father passed him on the way down through the air, getting a similar way through the song. This was obviously the tradition when jumping from

MacDonald's Bluff.

"Apparently," said Stephen, indicating a rock under the water further around the cape from where we were standing, "somebody tried jumping in over there when the sun was reflecting off the sea, and he couldn't see the rocks. Broke his arm in two places."

"What? Over there and over here?" I asked.

"No. Not two places like locations," explained Stephen, pointing to two different parts of his arm. "I mean here and here. But I wasn't going to say that to your mum, or she wouldn't have let us come."

I was letting this sink in and looking carefully at the dangerous rocks when I felt a rush of air behind me. I turned to see a red-capped blur leap off the cliff, and Stephen got all the way through *E-I-E-I-O* before his voice disappeared into the water. Inching my way towards the edge, I looked over to see his ginger hair pop back into view as he smiled up to me.

"It feels cold at first," he shouted while treading water, "but each jump afterwards is easier. It's your turn now, Neil. Oh, and don't forget to tuck your knees under when you hit the water, or the impact will push your giblets back up inside you."

Stephen had a lovely way with words.

Stalling for time, I took off my t-shirt and flip-flops.

"Come on, Neil!" called Stephen.

I couldn't see him, but I knew it was the moment to go for it. I took three quick breaths and ran for it. I too had intended to sing Old MacDonald, but the only sound that left my mouth as I leapt into the unknown was a terrified *Aaaaaaaargh!*

The descent was rapid and my stomach seemed high in my chest before the cold sea swallowed me whole. I momentarily regretted not having put on my goggles as I wasn't sure which way was back up to the surface. Just before panic kicked in, I started rising and kicked upwards. Gulping in air, I turned to see Stephen grinning at me.

"It's awesome, isn't it?" he said, beckoning me to swim over to him so that I'd be out of the drop zone if anyone else jumped off.

"It was pretty amazing," I answered as we swam back to the rocks.

We spent the next couple of hours making repeated jumps, singing *Old MacDonald* and laughing all the way; we mostly jumped separately but occasionally together. I was so glad that we'd refused the cultural trip with the adults. It was only when we both realised that we were very hungry that we noticed our fingers had wrinkled up like raisins. We decided to stop for the morning, go back to the apartment to change, and get some lunch at the poolside. With our towels around our shoulders, we recounted tales of our heroic leaps on the short journey back to the hotel. On arrival at the door, I stood aside to let Stephen through. He took the bag from me and rummaged around inside. Having found no trace of the key in there, he thrust his hands in the pockets of his shorts but again came up empty-handed apart from pulling out a very damp Queen of Spades with Black Widow on it.

"Where's the key, Stephen, and why have you got a playing card in your pocket?" I asked calmly.

"Er. Just give me a minute," he said, stalling and looking through the bag for a second time. I then noticed that he wasn't wearing his tuna cap either.

"And where's your cap?" I continued as he put his hand to his head to check that it really wasn't there.

My stomach rumbled, and Stephen looked up slowly to meet my eyes.

"I've got no idea, mate," he said solemnly. "Dad's going to kill me. And I'm starving too. Look at this," he said, running his finger up and down the side of his chest. "Not just one or two ribs visible. I'm showing full cage!"

"Okay. Let's retrace our steps," I said, thinking strategically. "Perhaps it fell out of the bag."

We followed our path back in the direction of the cape,

stopping only half-way up the slope of the cliff to collect the Iron Man Ace of Hearts that was lying in the grass at the side of the path. There was no sign of the key in the area around where we had left the bag, and we therefore began to panic that somebody might have stolen the key whilst we were in the sea. This was unlikely since the father and son who had been alternating their jumps with us for about half an hour seemed to be perfectly respectable, and there'd been nobody else around.

"Think back," I instructed Stephen. "Did you take off your cap before jumping in for the first time?"

"I'm not sure." He replied slowly.

"Okay," I said. "You search in the grass around here for the key while I go in the sea to look for the cap."

Stephen agreed forlornly, and I took my goggles and headed down the path to the rocks at the bottom of the cliff. It helped that I loved holding my breath and swimming underwater, so I swam out to roughly the spot where we had been entering the sea, took a deep breath and ducked my head down to check out the terrain. My goggles were pretty good, and, as luck would have it, the sea was relatively clear. A few rocks and stones dotted the mainly sandy seabed, and for some reason The Little Mermaid film that we had watched before coming on holiday came back to me. Among the stones, I caught sight of some patches of red, so I came back up for air before taking a great lungful and pushing down again. I swam down to the bottom and discovered that the red things I'd seen were the backs of playing cards; there were loads of them strewn around. I gathered as many as I could before coming back up to the surface for air.

"Stephen!" I called, holding up the eight or so soggy cards that I'd found and waiting for his face to appear at the cliff top. "Did you have the whole pack of cards in your shorts when you jumped in?"

"Maybe," he answered slowly and guiltily.

"Any luck with the key?" I asked, swimming over to

the rocks to put the cards onto a dry rock.

"Not yet," he answered before disappearing from view again.

My next few dives were fruitful; each time I came back up with another fistful of moist Marvel cards. Treading water at the surface in preparation for another attempt, I spotted a larger red shape a little further away. I manoeuvred myself in that direction and submerged myself again. My first instinct wasn't wrong: it was the tuna cap.

"Stephen!" I called again.

"Yes?" he replied, his face reappearing at the cliff top.

"Your cap is down here too," I shouted, waving it at him. "I've found about thirty-five cards and your cap. Did you put the key in your pocket too when your Dad gave it to you, you numpty?"

"Maybe," he answered again.

"Why don't you come down here and help then?" I suggested. "I bet the key is down here somewhere."

He clambered down the path to join me but said that he would be pretty useless in the sea without goggles of his own, and he was not great at holding his breath either. I took a quick break to get my strength back. It didn't help that we hadn't had lunch yet and that my energy levels were low. I thought of the iced buns that Wilberforce's mother always left for us when we were playing Dungeons and Dragons at their house. One of those would be perfect right now. I missed Wilberforce too.

Having rested for a few minutes, I pushed the thought of Mrs Pudge's buns aside and swam back into the water, deciding to try approaching from a different angle. I dived down and spotted a few more cards, which I collected before kicking back upwards. However, in turning my head, the reflection of something shiny caught my eye.

"There's something shiny down there!" I exclaimed, handing Stephen the fistful of cards I'd just recovered.

"Oh yes!" enthused Stephen. "Keep going, mate.

You've got this."

It took me a couple more attempts to find the same spot where I'd seen the metallic glint, but, sure enough, there was the key to the apartment, poking out from underneath the Incredible Hulk Ace of Clubs.

"Yes! You da man!" shouted Stephen triumphantly as I broke the surface, smiling and holding the little key aloft. I handed it to him carefully as I climbed out onto the rocks.

"Thank you from the heart of my bottom, mate," he added, letting out a crackling fart.

We counted the cards and found that we had forty-five. Two more that we had found in Stephen's pocket and on the grass verge meant that we were five short of a full deck, but I was too exhausted to dive down any more. We'd probably have to throw them all away anyway, but I didn't want to leave them in the sea for pollution reasons. Putting the wet cards in the bag, I took the key from Stephen before we headed back to the apartment, got changed and had a sandwich at the poolside. Mine was devoured in less than five minutes, and then we found two sun loungers in the shade of a parasol. I drifted off to sleep thinking that only Stephen could have jumped into the sea with a cap on, a key and a full pack of cards in his pocket, and not have noticed that he'd lost them all!

We'd have to stick to Top Trumps from now on.

CHAPTER 13

STEPHEN'S GIRLFRIEND

"Sorry about yesterday, mate and your cards. And thanks for not dobbing me in to Mum and Dad about the key," said Stephen as we made our way back from breakfast to the apartment.

"There's nothing to be sorry about," I replied. "It was a great day and certainly not a boring one. Cliff diving is so much fun. Anyway, they didn't ask; I didn't tell."

"I think I was just distracted thinking about Shamone," he continued. "I really want to give her a dose of the old STI."

"What on Earth is that?" I asked, confused.

"STI," he stated, spelling it out. "Severe Tongue Interaction. I'm ready to deploy my STI on her. I am the STI master! At least, I'm pretty sure I am, and today's my chance to prove it."

This conjured up an image that I hadn't really wanted to imagine and found hard to shake. I found myself wishing I could have had my memory erased like C-3PO. However, we'd agreed before breakfast that I was happy to hang out with the oldies for the morning to give the two love birds some time alone together. I was going to meet up with them after lunch, and Mum, Dad, Mike and Diana had decided last night that we would all go out into Cala Plata for dinner this evening rather than eating in the hotel. Lemony had moaned of course that she didn't see why she and Ella couldn't stay behind, but Dad had managed to persuade her by allowing her to stay out later for an extra hour.

*

"Do I smell of onions and garlic?" asked Stephen, testing his breath while looking at himself in the bathroom mirror. "I'm beginning to regret some of those tapas choices from dinner last night."

"No more than usual," I said reassuringly, sniffing close to him.

"I'd probably better clean my teeth twice just to be sure," he nodded.

"Good plan," I continued. "You might want to change your t-shirt too. You've had that one on for a couple of days now, and it's getting a bit stale in the pits."

"Thanks for the tip," replied Stephen, "but it's my favourite top. I'll give it an extra-long blast of Wild Tiger; that should do it."

Stephen's deodorant of choice was almost overpoweringly pungent, but he was a firm supporter of anything orange, and wild tigers were orange, so I knew there would be no changing his mind. He applied the spray to both his armpits and also directly to the t-shirt before running a cursory brush through his usually unruly ginger hair and declaring that he was ready for action.

"Looking sharp," I complimented.

"Too right," replied Stephen, making the final

adjustments in the mirror. "Even I fancy me. How's this for a swagger?" He showed me his special lady-killer walk.

"Perhaps not," I advised. "It looks as if you've got hip issues."

"Oh. Okay," he nodded.

Ignoring the inevitable "go, get her tiger!" from Mike and the proud hugs from Diana, Stephen pushed to the front door where I wished him good luck and confirmed that he and Shamone would come and join me after lunch if everything had gone well.

"Oh, and perhaps don't worry about converting her to Dungeons and Dragons just yet," I suggested, noticing his puzzled look as I pulled the door closed.

*

"Are you sure you'll be all right with just us this morning," asked Mum. "Do you want to go to the other pool bar area with Lemony and Ella?"

Lemony looked ready to protest, but I laughed before she had the chance, securing my goggles in place, throwing down my towel and rushing towards the pool.

"Don't worry about me, Mum," I shouted. "I'll be just fine."

With that, I dive bombed into the deep end and let myself drop all the way to the bottom. And indeed I was fine. I had fun in the Jacuzzi, trapping air in my shorts so that it looked as if I had an enormously swollen groin. I challenged myself to go further and further underwater without coming up for breath, passing underneath people in the deeper water. I played spies, trying to get up close to other guests and listen to their conversations without them knowing I was there. I also invented an underwater swimming game which I called Sharko Polo. I was still working on what you actually had to do, but the name was very pleasing. It mostly involved wriggling around in an attempt to propel myself forwards. Having Stephen there would have added an extra dimension to the game, but it was only one morning, and we still had a few days left to flesh out the rules together.

My wrinkled fingers indicated that it was probably time to get out of the water for a while, so I hopped out of the pool and dripped my way back to our base. Lemony and Ella were nowhere to be seen, of course, and the adults were either sunbathing or sleeping; it was difficult to tell. The spare lounger was in the shade, and I'd only been on it for a minute before goose pimples appeared on my arms like a Braille tattoo that read *I'm freezing*.

The base of the sunshade was heavy concrete, but I wanted to move it so that I could warm up in the sun. After a couple of futile heaves, a muscular arm passed into my vision and clasped the pole by the base; I looked up into the piercing blue eyes of Stijve Tepels.

"Don't strain your back, little man," he said quietly, so as not to disturb the slumbering parents. He showed a mouthful of white teeth as he smiled and easily lifted the parasol out of the way. "Now I go take care of your sister and her friend," he added, winking at me and strutting away.

Whether it was the 'little man' comment, the grin, the wink, the strut or something else, I knew that I didn't trust this guy at all. Not just because he was stupid enough to fancy Lemony, but I had a feeling he was up to something.

I was torn from my wondering by a sound like a wet slap against plastic. Looking round, I saw my mum restlessly changing position on her lounger and mumbling something to herself in her sleep.

Defensively, I checked to see if anybody had heard her little *Lady and the Trump* tummy squeak, but, thankfully, nobody had. The bookmark was still very near the start of her book, The Constant Headache, I noticed as I picked up my own Frank Beans story and settled down to read in the sun.

*

My good humour hadn't faded all morning or through lunch either, although I admit to being a little nervous as to what Shamone would be like and how this afternoon would go. I took a post-lunch stroll to the toilet and was just on my way back when I heard a familiar voice behind me.

"I'm back, amigo!" called Stephen.

I would usually have made a little quip back to Stephen, but I'll admit that it felt a bit awkward that Shamone was with him. A quick glance downwards told me that they were holding hands. I gulped. Stephen must have sensed my discomfort, so he casually let go of her hand by means of introducing us.

"Neil, Shamone. Shamone, Neil," he said.

She smiled at me, and we said hello to each other before she excused herself to go to the toilet.

As soon as she had disappeared from sight around the corner, Stephen let out a huge five-second fart. The relief on his face was plain to see.

"I've been holding that in for hours," he chuckled.

"What a gentleman," I replied, wafting the air in front of my face. "She's probably doing exactly the same in the toilets."

"No," he said sagely. "Girls don't fart. It's a known fact."

I pondered this as we sat on the edge of the pool with our legs dangling in the water, thinking that I didn't remember hearing Lemony fart, although that could have been because she spent as little time with me as possible. However, I'd definitely heard my mum doing it earlier on the sun lounger and also last Christmas. Perhaps it only happened when they were asleep, but that was a debate for another time.

"What do you think of her?" asked Stephen.

"She's a bit shrimpy," I answered.

135

"Petite is the word you're looking for," he corrected.

"No. I mean she smells of shrimps," I said.

"Oh that?" replied Stephen. "She had a prawn cocktail sandwich for lunch. She's very sophisticated."

"So, how did the morning go?" I asked.

"Amazing," he answered. "Honestly, the electricity between us would have been enough to power one of those very small bulbs we used on a circuit board in science lessons. And I even got some STI action."

"Smooth!" I said. "How did it happen?"

"To be honest, the conversation had sort of dried up a bit, so I just leaned over and went for it to fill the silence. It was either that or go back to Dungeons and Dragons, but I remembered your advice, so I took the plunge. We were probably going for about fifteen seconds before I had to stop to breathe."

I was very impressed that Stephen had taken this step towards manhood. He was clearly proud of himself but trying to remain cool.

"You can get quite a good seal when your lips are locked together," he continued. "It even ran through my mind whether I'd be able to suck air into *my* lungs through *her* nose, but I couldn't work that out."

"Wow," I said. "That's honestly what you were thinking about?"

"A combination of that, how to avoid snagging my tongue, lips and gums on her braces and also what to talk about when we'd finished snogging," he replied. "There was a lot going on in my head."

He pulled down his lower lip to show me a couple of sore, red spots on his gum where the washing machine technique had led to some collateral damage on her dental device. Who knew that romance was so involved? I wished that Cameron, Grub and Wilberforce could have been here too so that I wouldn't be the only one who wasn't kissing anybody.

"And did you manage to think of something else to say

to her?" I asked

"Compliments," he answered. "I told her that her hair reminded me of marble cake and that it was soft, strong and very long. She loved it. We saw that pool guy at one point. The weird thing was that he seemed to be flirting with someone who wasn't Lemony. I could tell because she had long dark hair, but she was facing away from us, so I couldn't make out who it was. Anyway, Shamone'll be back any minute, and I think I'll need to go to the loo too. Is it okay to leave you two together for a bit?"

"Oh," I replied, considering Stijve and wondering what to say, not having thought of the scenario of being alone with her. "What should we talk about? Did you learn anything else about her?"

"Her parents are called Michael and Lisa-Marie. I got that much but not a huge amount more," he said, glancing over my shoulder to where Shamone was obviously returning. "In fact, perhaps *you'll* be able to give *me* some more details later."

Thanks, Stephen!

My heart was thumping as Stephen explained that he was going to the toilet and would be back soon. Shamone sat down confidently next to me and then slid into the pool, turning to face me while hanging on to the side. A whirr of thoughts went through my mind as to what to say before one thing came out of my mouth that needed clearing up.

"I didn't poo in the pool while we were playing water polo, you know. That wasn't me."

"I know," she replied, smiling. "Stephen's told me all about you and that you always tell the truth. If you say that, it must be true. That's one of the reasons I like him: he's a very loyal friend. I think he's a deep person. I saw it in his eyes."

"No he's not," I answered, slipping into the water next to her. "He's very shallow actually. What you see is what you get, but that's a good thing. What you saw in his eyes is just bloodshot because he hasn't got goggles and was swimming underwater yesterday. He might have got PPI."

She giggled and tossed her head back just as Stephen came back from the toilet and climbed into the pool next to Shamone. Conversation flowed quite easily as we talked about the Sugar Tots club. We even agreed the rules for Sharko Polo and laughed as we played that for a long time. In fact, time flew, and it was hard to believe it was time to get ready for dinner when my dad came to fetch us. A look of disgusted amusement crossed Dad's face as Stephen pulled Shamone in for a shamelessly full-on goodbye snog.

Once he'd released her and she'd gulped down a lungful of air, she said goodbye to me and went to find her own parents. I suppose it was not as bad as I'd feared sharing Stephen with someone else. It was only for another full day anyway.

Then I'd have to pick up the pieces of Stephen.

CHAPTER 14

EATING OUT

We only had two nights left of our holiday, and this was the one night that we were going out of the resort to eat in a different restaurant. As we waited in the hotel lobby for Mike and Diana, I could see that it pained Dad to pay for an extra meal when the holiday was all inclusive; he was fiddling nervously with his shirt, checking his wallet every now and then. He looked smart, however, and Mum looked pretty too. She was even wearing perfume which reminded me of when I used to pull the best petals from the roses in our garden, mix them in a bucket of water and sell it to Mum as perfume. I'd called it Home Cologne.

Stephen had been persuaded to ditch his favourite fetid t-shirt in favour of wearing a more formal shirt, as had I, and Mum said we looked very dashing.

Lemony and Ella were over by the poster advertising tomorrow night's drag queen show, getting excited.

"Trixie Patel, Grotty De Boeuf and Butch Flaccidy. Are

you into the drag queens as well, Ella?" asked Mum, reading the poster over their shoulder and making polite conversation.

"Of course she is," interrupted Lemony before Ella had chance to answer. "But don't feel as if you have to come as well. There's a karaoke night in the bar which would be much more up your street."

"Did somebody say karaoke?" announced Mike who had now appeared in the lobby with Diana. "I'm up for that!"

He had slicked back his hair with some sort of gel and was wearing a stained shirt that was unbuttoned as far as his considerable belly.

"You look lovely, Diana," said Mum. "Red carpet ready."

I thought that description was pushing it a bit. Perhaps wearing a dress made her *night out in Cala Plata* ready, but not much more than that.

"Thanks, Emma," she smiled, "although my plus one's got muck all down his shirt."

She pointed to Mike and tried to dab at the stains.

"It's only me dinner medals," he answered, batting her away, "and I'm only going to make it worse later anyway."

"Oh, God," said Lemony before turning and leading us out of the hotel.

*

The low sun in another cloudless blue sky looked over us on our stroll through the town of Cala Plata. The port itself was pretty, but there were many tacky shops selling all sorts of crapola designed to trap tourists.

"You like?" asked a wizened old lady with a toothless grin, holding up a t-shirt announcing *I heart Cala Plata* from her little stall on the roadside. "Only twelve euro."

"No way," I replied, thinking about the small amount of money I'd managed to raise before coming on holiday.

"I've got the lowest clothing standards of anyone, and even I wouldn't wear that."

She put the t-shirt down and picked up a fridge magnet which was a relief map of the island. "Eight euro," she said in hope.

"You have to understand," I replied, "that twelve year olds don't want that sort of thing. Seriously, what am I supposed to do with a fridge magnet?"

Stephen grabbed my arm and ushered me onwards.

*

The neon sign outside the *El Pollo Hermano* restaurant looked new and expensive; Dad gulped as we approached. We all stepped around a pool of dried vomit on the pavement close by, which I hoped was not a review left by a previous diner.

"Buenas tardes!" greeted a waiter who was almost a spitting image of the flirtatious egg-man, Mario, from our hotel. They could almost have been brothers, so Stephen and I decided that he was called Luigi.

"Bonjour," replied Mike as we were shown to our table.

"You sit here, boss?" asked Luigi, jokingly acting as if I was the head of the family. As I sat down, he put his hand on my shoulder.

"I don't like that. It's too familiar," I stated. Luigi removed his hand and left us to consider our menus.

"I bet he gives you the bill at the end of the meal," said Stephen quietly.

"There is zero chance that won't happen," I smiled.

The menu was in Spanish with curious English translations underneath. Among the offerings were unfamiliar items such as *chicken with its crispy epididymis and a citrus slime*, *asparagus spume*, *aubergine stain*, *oily egg splat*, *squished potato*, and *incidental mental lentils*.

Thankfully, there was a simple burger and chips on the

menu, so I decided that would be a safer option. Mike was more adventurous.

"I was going to go for the *sketty bolonaise*," he announced, "but you're not on holiday every day. I'm going to try the exotic-sounding 'unmentionable sweetbreads'. Cadillards? Criad..? Callirads?"

"Criadillas," corrected Lemony with a smile.

"All right, pronounciation police," answered Mike.

"Actually, it's pro*nun*ciation police," replied Lemony, turning to chuckle about something with Ella.

Luigi came over to take the order, heading straight for me.

"I start with the big boss. What you want, my friend?"

"I'll have the burger and chips, please," I answered.

"Are you skin-on?"

I paused, unsure of how to answer, and was then appalled by this question.

"Whether or not I'm circumcised is none of your business!" I said indignantly.

Mum put her head in her hands while Lemony groaned and looked away. Stephen choked down half of the mouthful of water he had, laughing and spitting out the other half in a thin mist at the same time. Diana patted him on the back.

"No' the pipi. Your cheeps, boss," he replied calmly. "Skin-on wedgies or French fries?"

"Oh, yes," I blushed, understanding at last. "Wedgies please."

"Burger and cheeps for the boss man," he repeated, writing on his pad before turning to Mike. "You, sir?"

"Criadillers, see voo play," said Mike.

Luigi made a cupping action in the air with his hand. "That's the goat, yeah? Unmentionables?"

Mike nodded blankly before turning to Diana.

"Looks like there's some goat's cheese on it. Yum!"

Just as Dad finished ordering, Mike added to the waiter in a whisper, "Give il a spicy une!"

142

"I don't want a *spicy une*, thank you very much," protested Dad.

The rest of the group ordered in either a very feeble attempt at Spanish or else in slow and loud English, pointing condescendingly at the menu before Luigi finally got to Ella.

"And the preety lady?" asked Luigi.

At that moment, I realised that I couldn't recall ever having heard Ella's voice before. She may have been my sister's best friend and have spent a lot of time at our house, but Lemony always spoke for her, or they whispered together. I listened and could hardly believe my ears. What she said sounded to my untrained ear something like this:

"Hash terror fanajatala doss es pessy yalas eee parachutay polly pinchay sasha leekay thai kwando loss federer pinky chatter con bowler peshy poo."

"Who knew she was an idiot?" I whispered to Stephen.

However, Luigi smiled at her and said something equally strange back to her after which he left our table and went back to the kitchen. Everybody was looking at Ella.

"So she speaks Spanish. Get over it," said Lemony.

"How come you…" began Dad.

Ella was about to answer when Lemony interrupted again.

"She used to live in Spain. Her mum's Spanish. Now enough with the Spanish inquisition."

They then turned to talk to each other, and the matter was closed.

*

There was a good deal of friendly joking around the table including Mike announcing 'Let the chips fall where they may' after Stephen had dropped a couple of his on the floor. Even Dad managed to loosen up and seemed to have accepted the prospect of paying for an extra meal, although I did notice that he kept a very close eye on how much wine there was left in the bottle. I think he was pouring small amounts so that he wouldn't need to order an extra bottle. Mike seemed to be happily declaring how tasty his meal was while frequently picking bits of it from between his teeth.

I was not happy with my food and was ready to say something to Luigi when he came to our table. However, his question of whether or not we wanted dessert was met with a very swift 'no' from Dad, and he disappeared off to fetch the bill before I had chance to speak.

Eventually, he came back, and, just as Stephen had predicted, passed the bill to me with a grin and a wink.

"Here you go, boss man. You pay the beel?"

As Stephen grinned at me, Luigi laughed to himself before passing it to my dad. Dad gulped.

"How was everything?" Luigi asked.

"I'm glad you asked that," I began before anyone else could answer. "The burger meat was fatty and the chips were undercooked. And there was something weird on the salad."

"That was dressing," answered Luigi.

"Dressing doesn't wriggle," I said, turning over a salad leaf to show what looked like a small maggot.

"Grub!" exclaimed Stephen. "He's with us in spirit."

Anyway, Luigi inspected my plate before finally agreeing to give us a discount which made my dad very happy. He patted me on the shoulders and gave me a big smile. As Dad was paying, Luigi smiled across to Mike.

"How your balls, my friend?"

Lemony and Ella chuckled together as Mike looked puzzled.

"Criadillas," explained Luigi, making the same cupping gesture as before. "They are goat's balls, you understand?"

Mike looked crestfallen before laughing nervously as he realised what he had just eaten. As we stood up to leave, I noticed that he took a swig of water, swirled it round his mouth and then spat it back into the glass. I overheard him saying to Diana that maybe he would be better sticking to the *sketty bolonaise* in future.

As we left the *El Pollo Hermano* restaurant, I stepped over the dry vomit pool, wondering if that was the result of another order of criadillas from an unsuspecting guest.

*

It had been an exhausting day. Stephen talked about Shamone for the whole of the walk back to the hotel. We only had one full day left in Cala Plata, and I knew that he wanted to spend some of that day with her, no doubt alone.

After we'd returned to our room, we got changed and lay on our beds staring at the ceiling.

"One more day with Shamone," sighed Stephen, "and then she goes back to Egypt and I go back to Lower Piercing. Why does love have to be so hard, Neil?"

"You're not really asking an expert," I replied.

Just then a strange desire to level with Stephen came over me. After all, he was my best friend, and he'd told me everything about his feelings for Shamone.

"You know, mate. I think that even though it hasn't lasted a long time, you've really got a lot out of being with Shamone. We can't stay young forever, and you've opened up to new experiences. I'm sure you'll be the better man for it. Also, I should probably have told you earlier…much earlier…but I've had a crush on someone for a while too. I haven't dared say anything because I didn't really understand my feelings. I still don't, but whenever she's around, I get butterflies in my tummy. It's Fleur, Stephen. She's the one. Is it like that with you and Shamone? Is that the way she makes you feel?"

I breathed out, aware that pouring my heart out like this had made my cheeks flush red. At the same time, I felt relief at sharing this with somebody. That somebody was my best friend, so I knew he wouldn't betray me. He'd listen and give me some good advice.

"So, what should I do about it when we get back to school, Stephen?" I asked.

He didn't reply.

"Stephen?"

I stopped staring at the ceiling and looked over towards him, propping myself up on my elbow.

He was fast asleep.

CHAPTER 15

LONELY GUY AT THE BAR

From the moment we woke up, all through breakfast, and down at the pool, Stephen talked about little else other than Shamone Eehi. It was clear that he'd fallen asleep before hearing a word of what I'd said about Fleur the night before, but my bravery in revealing my secret had faded away into doubt about whether it was the right thing to share or not.

My expression must have betrayed a bit of boredom after hearing how wonderful Shamone was for the umpteenth time and failing to answer the question about how a distance relationship could work between two twelve year olds who lived two and a half thousand miles apart.

"Am I going on about it?" asked Stephen.

"You are a bit," I answered. "Especially since it's our last full day here."

"Sorry, mate," he shrugged. "But it's my last day with her too. And I'm not thinking about it all of the time, just most of the time."

Sure enough Stephen tried his best to concentrate on having fun with me, but I could tell that with every break in play during Sharko Polo, he'd be looking around in case Shamone was there. She'd gone out for most of the day with her parents and probably wouldn't be back until the early evening.

The extra intense application of Wild Tiger before dinner confirmed to me that Stephen was planning to meet up with Shamone as soon as we'd eaten and spend his final evening with her. This was hardly the barnstorming finish to the holiday that I'd wished for, but, once again, I had to come to terms with this sharing business. If I said anything to Stephen, it would only upset his evening too. I was going to have to put a positive spin on an evening with the parents. I figured that Lemony and Ella would be off with Stijve somewhere, but I'd forgotten that tonight was the drag show extravaganza to which they rushed off with great excitement. They'd even doused themselves in outrageous make-up for the occasion, and I'm pretty sure I caught sight of Lemony smiling at one point.

The main courtyard of the hotel was a central hub from which several entertainment areas could be accessed. There were bars, large lounges, performance spaces with stages and the hotel's own night club.

Some teams must have been doing a football because one of the bars had turned into a sports bar where a crowd had gathered around a large screen shouting at the players to 'use it', 'line it', or 'get him off'. Despite the volume of their shouts, of course the players couldn't hear this incisive advice, but it gave the sunburnt viewers something to say between their swigs of beer. I couldn't quite hear properly, but it also seemed that they thought the referee must have enjoyed winking as much as Stijve Tepels, who, I noted, was also there in his own clothes rather than the hotel uniform. It must have been his night off. He looked around and met my eye, raising his eyebrows and winking before turning back to the action on screen. I got the impression that Dad was about to suggest joining that group when he caught Mum's stern look, and she suggested the karaoke bar.

"Actually, I've got a date," announced Stephen, earning 'oohs' and grins from the adults.

"Sorry, mate," he continued turning aside to me. "I'll try not to be too long, but, you know, she does love getting the STI from the master."

One man hug later, he was off to find his girl while I followed the adults over to the karaoke bar. In no time at all, Mike had grabbed the song list and flicked through until delight spread across his face upon finding the song he wanted. He barely had time to shout to my dad that he wanted a lager before he was up on stage with a microphone in his hand.

The familiar brassy introduction to *New York, New York* began as Mum, Dad and Diana looked on expectantly. I felt a cringe of embarrassment on absent Stephen's behalf.

"Start spreading *manure*…" sang Mike. Diana burst out her machine-gun laugh.

"That's classic Mike," she shouted, "always changing the words."

It was all a bit too much for me.

"I might go and sit in one of the quieter bars for a while and then go and watch something on TV back in the room," I said to Mum.

"Are you okay, Poppet? Do you want me to come with you?" she asked, looking concerned.

"No. Don't worry. It's not how I wanted to spend the last evening, but *c'est la vie*," I replied.

She leaned over to explain to Diana and ask for the key to our room. While Diana fiddled around in her handbag, I got to appreciate a little more of Mike's singing. I'm not sure if he was sharp or flat, but he was definitely one of them and very much so.

"Come back and join us whenever you like," consoled

Mum, rubbing my arm affectionately.

Wandering back into the courtyard, I noticed smiles and laughter coming from everybody. Bustling along or sitting and chatting, everyone was happy except me. One of the bars caught my attention because it looked quieter than the rest. I may have been a bit young to be going to a bar on my own, but heading straight up to the room for the whole evening seemed as if I'd be admitting defeat.

A bar tender in a white shirt and black waistcoat was looking across the courtyard straight at me, a small, welcoming smile on his face. He had a bald head and a beard, as if his head was on upside down. I trudged over and sat down on a stool, observing that his eyes never left me as if he could see nobody else. He was wiping a glass very thoroughly and noticed me gazing at what he was doing.

"Each guest should be able to experience a perfect shine on their glass. The shining is a most important part of the service we provide here. What'll it be, traveller?" he asked, his English accent standing out as unusual among the hotel staff.

I ordered a lemonade and helped myself to the complimentary salted peanuts while he prepared my drink. After the first few, I started to throw them up and catch them in my mouth until one landed in my eye, the salt causing me to grimace and try to blink through the sharp sting. I went back to placing them in my mouth.

"So what brings you to Rick's bar?" he asked, setting down the drink precisely on a coaster in front of me.

I felt quite grown up in spite of my disappointment, stirring the ice cubes around with a plastic stick.

"Things aren't going so well for me tonight, and I feel lonely," I said.

"I usually tell my guests that the answer doesn't lie at the bottom of a glass," he advised, "but since you're drinking lemonade, that will only get you to the Gents' rather than give you a hangover, so if you want to tell me about your journey, I'm a good listener."

He spoke softly and reassuringly in a way that inspired trust, so I told him all about the situation with how I'd known Stephen since before primary school and how Shamone had come between us.

"Hmm. And now you feel left out," Rick pondered, stroking his beard.

"It's not that I feel left out, just excluded," I said, looking imploringly at him for the mystic wisdom I felt sure that he would provide.

"Well," he began, "your fellow traveller is taking steps along his own path with this girl. It is the first time for you to share him with another. This is a difficult time for a young man, but every explorer must forge his own trail. It's up to you to write your own script as he must write his, but it doesn't mean you won't share many scenes together in this play we call life."

Rick may have been talking in a flowery way, but what he was saying soothed me.

"You're right," I sighed. "It's not easy, but I feel better already; after all, it's just one more evening."

"Indeed," he smiled, never taking his eyes from mine. "You've come a long way since leaving Prince Albert. Who knows what else you'll discover starting from this very evening?"

"But how did you...?" I began. I didn't understand. I'd mentioned knowing Stephen since primary school, but I hadn't told him that the school was called Prince Albert back in Lower Piercing.

He continued to stare into my eyes, smiling knowingly. I shifted on my stool to remind myself that there was a busy hotel courtyard behind me. I'd become so mesmerised by my conversation with Rick that I'd shut out the rest of the world from my thoughts. Who was this bar tender, and how did he know so much? I thought it would be best just to take a look around to clear my head, so I turned around in a slow circle to see all of the other guests which pulled me back to reality.

Turning back to the bar, I found no sign of Rick. A young lady was serving another guest further up the bar from me.

What had just happened?

Was it just my mind playing tricks on me?

Had Rick ever even been there?

The lady came over to me and asked if the lemonade was to be charged to my room or if I was paying.

"Wait a moment," I interrupted. "Where's Rick?"

"Who's Rick?" she asked. "There's no Rick who works here."

I was baffled and a little scared. Bizarre things like this didn't happen to me. Grub once swore that he'd seen a ghost in his garden one winter, but that turned out to be his dad dressing as Father Christmas in an attempt to keep the Christmas traditions going for longer.

My jaw dropped open, and I looked around again, panicking that I didn't know if it was the real life or just fantasy. I was caught in a landslide with no escape from reality.

Just then, my eyes opened wide in horror as Rick (or not Rick)'s head slowly emerged from below the bar, again still staring at me as he stood to his full height. I wasn't sure if the lady could even see him.

"How many people can you see at this bar?" I asked her slowly and quietly, not taking my eyes off not-Rick. I was terrified now.

"What are you talking about?" she asked.

"Don't be alarmed, traveller," said not-Rick calmly. "I assure you that everything is in order."

I stifled a scream, still not able to take my eyes from him and his faint, knowing smile. He turned his gaze slowly away from me and towards the bar tender lady. Horrified thoughts came to my mind about what he might do to her, if he was even human.

"Dishwasher's full, so I've put it on, Sandra," said not-

Rick.

I must admit that this was not as frightening a thing for him to say or do as I had expected.

"Thanks, Hugo," she answered.

"So, you can see him too?" I asked her, my foggy mind still not able to understand what was happening.

"Of course I can," she replied, looking confused. "Are you okay?"

"I don't know," I responded, my heart pounding in my chest. "Are you Rick?"

"This is Rick's bar," he said pointing above his head to the neon sign, "but my name is Hugo."

"But how did you know about Prince Albert?" I asked.

"I watched you leaving it," he answered, beginning to scare me again. Had he been in Lower Piercing last year? Who was this man?

By means of explanation, he pointed over my shoulder. I hesitated to take my eyes away from him, but I eventually dared to look back. Hugo (not-Rick) had been indicating the karaoke bar where my parents were. A small plaque by the entrance declared the bar to be called the Prince Albert. An odd coincidence which I was taking a while to process. Was this man simply a normal chap called Hugo who had seen me leaving a karaoke bar that happened to have the same name as my primary school? Had he just kindly offered me some advice before bending down to deal with a dishwasher? This seemed very hard to believe when all of the evidence pointed to a spectral being that could read my thoughts and make the universe disappear except for the spiritual plane that only we inhabited.

Either way, my head was spinning, and I needed some air. Without thinking about it, I gave our room number then stood and headed towards the exit. Once outside, I staggered onto a lawn that was being watered by a rotary sprinkler. I didn't care if I got wet; in fact, it might even have done me some good. However, the watering had made the surface slippery, and I lost my footing and fell face down into a flower bed.

CHAPTER 16

SWIMMING POOL DISCOVERY

The faint sound of music and laughter reached my ears as I pulled myself to my knees. My face, arms, knees and shirt were covered in mud. It may have been summer in a hot country, but the nightly sprinkler watering had made the earth very wet. What I could hear seemed to be coming from the drag show. There were a lot of lights and sparkles from inside. I stood up and walked over to the window where one of the queens seemed to be lip syncing to a song while wearing an outfit that was covered in yellow and green scouring sponges. At one point, she even jumped in the air and landed in the splits which looked very painful.

Casting my eyes over the audience, I eventually spotted Lemony who was clapping and singing along in a way she would never have done if she'd realised I was watching. Such was my confusion that I barely noticed that Ella didn't seem to be sitting with her.

"Are you here for the conference?" said a voice next to

me.

Turning my head, I could just about make out a man's features from behind a cloud of cigarette smoke. Immediately, all of the school talks we'd had came back to mind, and my internal stranger danger alarm went off. The advice as to what to do in such a situation was temporarily foggy, but I'm pretty sure it was to sprint in the opposite direction, so that's what I did, calling back to him over my shoulder:

"Of course I'm not here for a conference. Twelve year olds don't go to conferences."

I continued to run towards the main hotel, panting as I reached the lobby. Next to the stairs, I noticed a lift that seemed to go up to our floor. We hadn't seen this before, taking the stairs every time like suckers. My thoughts and emotions were running wild as I pressed the call button and waited. Finally, the doors opened and I got inside, longing for the sanctity of our apartment.

It was unusual to hear a broad Yorkshire male accent announce *guing oop* rather than any other elevator speech I'd ever heard before, but that also barely registered with me. The relief was so sweet when I eventually found our room and pulled out the key. I was just about to go inside when I noticed that the door to the next room where Mum and Dad were staying with Lemony and Ella was ajar. Had they forgotten to close it properly?

I pushed it open and entered cautiously, calling their names. The lights were off, so I tiptoed around and checked the apartment. Everything seemed normal, although the girls' room was very messy. There were clothes all over the floor, make-up scattered across the table, open suitcases and duvets and pillows in bulky clusters across the beds, even what looked like a dark wig strewn across one pillow with other wigs on the floor. Something to do with the drag show perhaps? Shrugging my shoulders, I left the apartment, closing the door properly this time and entering our own apartment.

I flicked on the lights and looked at myself in the full-length mirror in the lounge. I was filthy from head to toe. My dad had read a series of books where the main character was an assassin who always turned up the shower as hot as it would go after he had been on a stressful mission. It seemed to bring him back to a calm state, and if it was good enough for Urchin X, it was good enough for me.

I stripped off my muddy clothes and started the shower running with the temperature handle turned as far to the red as it would go. The steam was already filling the bathroom and relaxing me as I stepped under the water. I was under the hot jet for a fraction of a second before screaming a rude word very loudly and leaping back out. What a bloody stupid, ridiculous idea that was. Why would anyone scorch themselves? That doesn't make you feel better at all. I almost thought of suing the author of those books for planting such ideas in people's heads.

Once the shower was back to a sensible temperature, I stepped back under the water and let it wash over me. Deep breaths helped me to calm down from the over-excitement of the last half hour. I tried to convince myself that nothing unusual had really happened and that I had misinterpreted what was going on at Rick's bar. I watched a bit of TV in my dressing gown, but the only channel in English was showing boring news, so I decided to get dressed again and head down to see if the karaoke evening might have improved or if Stephen might have returned from his date.

Things were a little quieter in the central courtyard now, and the football match must have finished because the sports bar was much less lively with fewer people around. My natural curiosity was tempting me to glance over towards Rick's bar to see if Hugo was there, but I fought the urge and deliberately looked the other way to where the exit to the pool was.

Among the people milling around, I caught a glimpse

of familiar dark blond dreadlocks. Seeing Stijve Tepels again would not normally have interested me at all except for the fact that he was clearly not alone. He had his arm around the waist of a tall girl with dark straight hair, and they were heading out of the door. This girl was definitely not Lemony!

Once again, this evening had taken a turn towards the stressful. What was going on? The karaoke bar would have to wait while I investigated a bit further, so I cautiously made my way towards the same exit, pushed the door open and slipped outside.

The silhouettes of Stijve and this mystery girl were heading in the direction of the La Casita bar. I wanted to keep a safe distance away from them so that I could observe them without being seen, but I failed to cushion the closing door which made a banging sound behind me. I just had time to see the shadowy heads turn in my direction as I ducked down behind a large barrel that was serving as a container for a small palm tree.

Phew! That was a close one.

I counted to ten and then poked my head out. Since there was nobody to be seen, I crept along the route that they had taken and stopped at the edge of the swimming pool. Here, there was a shed that was used to store loungers and parasols, and La Casita was around the other side of it. I pressed my back to the shed and edged along. Risking a look around the corner, I spotted the tall girl disappearing either into the staff area or around the back of La Casita where Stijve had once taken Lemony. There was something familiar about this girl, but Stijve must have been in front of her because I couldn't see him. Although I didn't have an elaborate plan, I wanted to confront him and catch them red-handed. Bravery had been much easier to find when I'd had Stephen, Grub, Cameron and Wilberforce with me to fool Basher Walker and Batesy. Nevertheless, some courage stirred inside me, and I strode out from my cover to find that Stijve was not with the girl at all; he had been waiting for me behind the other side of the shed. He'd obviously spotted me earlier and stepped out to confront me.

"Where are you going, little man?" he asked, folding his arms in front of him and adopting a strong pose.

I was very intimidated, and all that came out of my mouth was a kind of squeak.

"What's the matter?" he continued, taking a step towards me. "And why are you sneaking around out here all alone?"

I gulped and finally found my voice.

"You're the one who's sneaking around. Who's that girl you're with?" I asked, waving an accusatory finger in the general direction of the bar.

"Her?" answered Stijve coolly with an arrogant smile. "Oh she's my sister. I'm just showing her around. Anyway, it's none of your business."

"But it is my sister's business," I replied. "You're supposed to be in love with her."

"Slow down, little man," laughed Stijve. "We only met this week. Nobody's in love with anybody."

Perhaps I didn't understand how quickly people fell in love, but I could spot a liar when I saw one.

"Well, I don't believe that that girl is your sister, and Lemony deserves to know if you're with somebody else," I said, my voice gaining strength as I felt confident that I was doing the right thing.

"You can believe what you want," said Stijve taking another step towards me. We were now within touching distance of each other. "But I know that it's no use you telling her anything; she doesn't even like you. I'd tell her you were making it up, and she'd believe me."

"Lemony knows I wouldn't lie to her!" I exclaimed.

"She hates you. You don't know her at all," he said, pushing me back by the shoulder menacingly. "I know she's watching the drag queens tonight, so why don't you leave your sister alone and go and play with your ginger friend. I'm going to look after my sister."

With that, he winked at me and then turned to walk casually towards the La Casita bar. It crossed my mind that in terms of who might believe what, Stijve certainly did not know me. It would be his word against mine.

*

I turned and sprinted back inside, crossing the courtyard to the entrance of the entertainment lounge where the drag show was taking place. The presence of a stocky man in a dark suit standing in front of the closed doors made me skid to a halt.

"Slow down, young fellow," said the man, spreading his hands to block my path. "Are you in a rush?"

"More of a hurry than a rush," I answered, panting for breath.

"Well you'd better show me your ticket then," he continued.

"But I haven't got one," I gasped.

"Okay. Well, let me tell you the long story about how you have to have a ticket to come in," he said condescendingly.

"Could you start nearer the end of the story?" I asked. "I really am in a hurry."

"You must really like drag queens," he smiled, folding his arms but not moving from in front of the doors. "However, you need a ticket to get in. That's the way it is."

"Oh please! Look, I really don't want to see the show," I spluttered in desperation. "I just need to speak to my sister who's in there watching it with her friend. She's the one wearing outrageous make-up."

"Look, pal," He replied. "Everybody in there is wearing outrageous make-up. What's she wearing?"

I could see that he might have been softening his attitude towards me.

"A yellow dress!" I pleaded. "Shoulder-length brown

hair."

"Okay. I think I know who you mean," he conceded. "You've got sixty seconds in there. She's over on the right. Oh and keep your head down. If those drag queens see you moving, they'll have you up on stage before you know it."

"Thank you!" I said genuinely as he opened the door for me.

I already knew where Lemony was sitting because of having seen her through the window earlier. Two drag queens in flamboyant costumes, one dressed as an angel, one as a devil, were insulting each other on stage using some words I did know, some I'd never heard before, and some I don't care to repeat. Heeding the bouncer's advice, I crouched down and scuttled my way over to Lemony. There was a spare seat right next to her, so I jumped into it.

The surprise on her face of having someone sit next to her soon faded into a scowl when she realised it was me.

"What are you doing here?" she spat through closed teeth.

"You have to listen to me for a moment, Lemony. It's important," I begged. "It's about Stijve, the pool waiter."

A look of horror appeared on her face. She was about to explode at me, but I held my nerve and spoke quickly before she had the chance.

"I know it's none of my business, but I wouldn't be here unless it was serious, would I?"

Lemony continued to stare at me, one of her nostrils twitching once to allow me to go on.

I gathered myself and explained. "He knows you're in here watching the show tonight, and he's with another girl. I saw them. She had long dark hair, and he had his arm around her, and they were going round the back of the La Casita bar together. He said she was his sister, but I'm sure she isn't. You've got to come with me to catch him red-handed."

Lemony's eyes darted fleetingly to the side and back as she considered my words.

"Look," she whispered. "I don't know what you're trying to prove, but you don't know what you're talking about."

I glanced over at the bouncer who was looking back at me and tapping his watch to say that my time had run out. I looked to the other side of Lemony to see if Ella had heard what I'd said and would agree with me. However, Lemony was next to an aisle. I must have been sitting in Ella's place.

"Where's Ella?" I asked, a sinking feeling growing in my stomach.

"She's got a headache," replied Lemony curtly. "She hasn't been here all evening."

An uncomfortable thought came to my mind, and I got up and walked towards the bouncer.

"You haven't had enough already, have you?" cackled one of the drag queens on stage suddenly. I realised she was talking to me. "We haven't finished yet. Quick, Butch. Go and chase him. Let's have him up on stage!"

The one with the devil costume began to rush down the stage steps towards me.

"Not today, Satan!" I shouted, sprinting towards the bouncer and out through the door beyond the reach of the outstretched arms of Butch Flaccidy.

I momentarily considered going into the Prince Albert karaoke bar to get my parents to help, but the chorus of Sweet Caroline by Neil Diamond being sung very badly told me that they were still busy in there and that getting Mike to leave would take time that I didn't have. If Lemony wasn't going to come with me, I'd do this by myself.

What happened in the dark was going to come to light…

CHAPTER 17

GAME OVER, PLAYER ONE

A brief stop in my room to get my torch and disposable camera was all I needed. The *Guing darn* lift voice in the Yorkshire accent would have charmed me under other circumstances, but I had to stay focused. I was going into the danger zone, and I was going alone.

It was a still evening with no breeze whatsoever. If you'd wanted wind, you'd have had to make it or break it yourself. This really was a make or break situation. I crept, ninja style, around the pool in the direction of the La Casita bar, determined not to make any noise this time. There could be no mistakes; I would only get one shot at getting evidence. As I approached, soft music reached my ears, and there was a faint light coming from behind the bar. I inched my way around the side of the building until I could peer around the corner. The bar backed onto the beach, and I could see two chairs set out facing the sea. Two figures, one of which sported thick dreadlocks, were in the seats, but they were wrapped up in each other, kissing passionately. Sister my arse!

There was too much distance from the bar to the chairs for me to be able to snap a photo of them from the front, but I spied a sturdy tree that was leaning directly above the double-crossing Dutchman and his squeeze. The player on the playa was about to get his comeuppance.

The waves were lapping on the shore as waves tend to do. That gentle noise coupled with the light music that was playing would allow me not to have to be ultra silent as I stepped up onto the first branches. Sweat started to bead on my skin as I slowly inched higher and then along the branch that was directly over their heads.

The two of them eventually unlocked their lips and picked up their drinks from the tree stump they were using as a table. I was directly overhead now, slowly moving my hand towards the pocket where my camera was stashed.

"What if he tells her, Stijve?" asked the girl. I thought I recognised this voice from somewhere but couldn't place it. I'd never heard Ella speaking English before, but still my suspicion that Lemony's best friend was betraying her was growing all the time. How could she do this? Stephen, Grub and Cameron would never have done this to me. This was breaking girl code, guy code, and probably even Morse code. Whatever the code: she was breaking it.

"He won't say anything, so relax," answered Stijve soothingly, slipping his arm back around the girl's shoulders. "Tonight is just for you and me."

My hand closed around the camera as a drop of sweat trickled down my forehead and paused on the end of my nose. I didn't dare move but tried to stick out my tongue to catch it before it fell. Alas, I was too slow, and my sweat dripped directly into Stijve's beer glass. Thankfully, he didn't hear the soft plop and raised his glass to his lips, taking a deep draft of sweat-infused beer. Take that, Tepels! However, I was perched precariously on this branch, and I needed one good photo for evidence.

The couple began kissing again, and my mind started racing, realising that perhaps I hadn't thought through the finer details of how I would actually get the photograph. I was quite high up on this branch, and I was unlikely to be able to swing from it with one hand while snapping off a shot with the other. That was option one out of the window. My second thought was to leap acrobatically to the sand and click the shutter before they knew what was happening. I discounted that pretty quickly after remembering what Mr Ashley had said about coordination in my school PE report. How I wished that my friends, or at least just Stephen, had been with me to discuss tactics. Our plan to defeat the bullies earlier in the summer had been perfected by everybody chipping in ideas. This time it was just me, and I'd rushed in without thinking clearly.

Camera in hand, my anxiety about what to do was rising, and I was beginning to think that my best move would be to climb back down the tree and rush out at them anyway. However, before I had chance to pursue that train of thought, another bead of sweat formed in my hairline and trickled down off the end of my nose. This one did not land in anyone's drink but fell right onto Stijve's closed eyelid. He didn't stop the kiss but angled his face upwards and opened his eyes.

SNAP!

I pressed the button on the camera and the flash went off. The perfect shot! In my attempt to slide the camera back into my pocket, I lost my grip on the branch and slipped. I managed to dangle helplessly from the branch for a second or two before falling flat onto my back on the sand below. The camera bounced out of my reach.

"Ouch. My bones!" I cried, reaching around to rub my sore back.

"Are you okay?" said the girl who was standing over me. I looked up, not into the face of Ella, but Ann Francisco, the Sugar Tots club host! "What were you doing up there? Wait, I remember you. You came to the club the other day."

"Ah, little man," said Stijve also looking down on me. "You just don't know when to quit, do you?"

"It's too late," I whimpered, pulling myself up onto my elbows. "I've got a photo now as evidence."

"You stupid little man," he mocked, picking up my camera. "This is a disposable camera – old school. You have to get the film developed, and there's no way to do that at the hotel. Also, you are leaving tomorrow, so you could only show Lemony the photo when you're back in England. What would I care about that? And one more thing. The camera is disposable."

He gripped the plastic device in both strong hands and twisted it until it snapped in half. I reached up despairingly towards him as he threw both pieces of the broken camera into the sea.

"There. I've disposed of it. Now, I'm pretty busy here with my hands full, little man," gloated Stijve, nodding to Ann and then turning fierce, "so you'd better understand that this is the last time I'll ask you to get lost before somebody gets badly hurt!"

I barely had time to become properly scared before a flash of yellow streaked across my vision behind Stijve. He collapsed to his knees with a pained shout.

"I'm badly hurt!" he cried, clutching his kneepits and turning onto his back to look up into the furious face of Lemony. She must have whacked him in the back of the knees forcing him to lose his balance and topple over. Ann Francisco looked at Lemony's savage expression before shaking her head and turning to run away. She may have been a couple of years older than my sister, but she knew well enough when it was better to save yourself.

"Oh, there you are, Lemony. Let me explain," stammered Stijve. "I'm glad your show has finished. Now we can spend your last evening together. I was just telling your brother how sad I was that you were busy."

He held his hand out towards her and gave her a smile

and a wink. A rush of blood came to my head.

"No you weren't. You were snogging the face off Ann Francisco! Admit it. There's no point changing tables on the Titanic. You're sunk."

"Sweet Lemony," said Stijve, rising to his knees. "Who are you going to believe? Me or the little man with the big imagination?"

"Obviously, I believe Neil," she spat before swinging her leg back and giving him a mighty kick in the pain palace. He let out a whimper and collapsed back into the sand, clutching his groin. Better to count the *criadillas* than rub the *criadillas*, I thought to myself, smiling.

My back wasn't badly hurt, so I got to my feet and stood by my sister. Lemony spent another few seconds looming over Stijve before stomping off further around the beach. Pride was beginning to rise in me as I lit up my torch and began to head back to the poolside. I hadn't got more than a few steps before my beam of light flashed on the faces of my parents, Mike, and Diana.

"Neil! What are you doing here? What's going on? Are you okay? Who's that on the floor, and where's Lemony?" asked Mum.

"Don't worry, Mum," I said calmly. "It's all sorted now. That's the pool boy. He'd been giving Lemony the old STI for most of this week, but I thought he was up to no good, so I followed him and caught him red-handed giving some STI to another girl. He's probably passing it around the whole hotel. Lemony was furious."

"Ew!" said Diana.

"Strewth!" said Dad.

"Well I never," said Mike.

"My poor baby," said Mum. "You're not supposed to see that sort of thing yet! And Lemony! She's still only..."

"Don't worry, Mum," I interrupted. "I'm twelve years old now. Stephen's doing the same on his date, I'm sure."

They all looked totally shocked and pulled strange faces which made me wonder how times had changed if they thought that twelve year olds kissing was unusual.

"We should go straight to the hotel manager to report this guy," suggested Dad firmly.

"Good idea," I said. "Oh, just one other thing. How did you know I was here?"

"Well," said Mum. "We got back to the apartments and found nobody in either of them. Ella had a terrible migraine headache, so she'd taken the key and gone back to bed. I was singing at the time, so your father told her just to leave the door ajar so that we could get back in. It wasn't the best suggestion in terms of security, but, well, you know, he'd had some beer."

Dad looked at his shoes sheepishly.

"Anyway," continued Mum, "we got back and both doors were locked, so we came to look for any of you. We saw Ella running away from here, but she darted off in a different direction when we called to her. Very strange, and we were surprised that she'd recovered from her migraine so quickly. We came to where she'd just been, and here we are. We didn't realise you were up to your heroics again."

"That wasn't Ella," I said. "I thought it was at first too, but it was the girl from Sugar Tots who just looks like her. I did think it was weird that Ella might have been kissing the same boy as Lemony."

At this point I began to wonder if the wig I'd seen on the pillow in Lemony and Ella's room might actually have been Ella's real head. Perhaps she hadn't answered me because of her headache.

"Right," said Dad. "First things first. Let's go and report this toe rag of a pool boy to the management, and then head up to bed."

"Yes," echoed Mike. "Come on, Neil. I'm sure Stephen's up there waiting for you and wondering where we all are."

"I'll be up in a bit," I replied. "There's one more thing I need to do first."

"What's that, love?" asked Mum.

"I need to check that my sister's okay."

With that, I turned away from my stunned parents and walked past Stijve, who was still cradling his pulverised plums, across the beach to where a lonely figure sat on the sand looking out at the sea.

CHAPTER 18

THE END OF LOVE

A clear-skied twilight over a beautiful beach made a perfect picture postcard image, but I had too important a job to do here to appreciate it fully. My sister was hurt and embarrassed, probably more so because it had happened in front of me. As I strode across the sand towards her, I realised that I did actually love Lemony even though she ignored me, belittled me in public and private, insulted my friends, tried to sabotage my toys, bullied me, hurt me physically, never showed that she cared for me, wished I hadn't been born, and was generally mean whenever there was an opportunity (and also sometimes when there didn't seem to be the slightest opportunity). Somehow, the brother-sister bond went deeper than all of that. At least, it did for me.

Wide logs had been placed along this part of the shoreline, and I sat myself down on one, leaving two free between Lemony and me.

"Go away, Neil," she said quietly without even looking

up to see that it was me.

"I just want to sit with you for a while," I replied, "to see that you're okay."

"Of course I'm okay!" she hissed. "Why on Earth would I not be okay?"

"I know you're cross at the moment," I began.

"Oh here it comes," she cried. "The village idiot speaks! You know exactly how I feel."

"Well, no," I said, "but I could listen."

"Do you honestly think I'd talk to you of all people, you little…" she said, preparing a tirade.

"Calm down," I interrupted. "Sticks and stones may break my bones, but calling names won't hurt me."

"Well that's good for you then because you're a $£*%&."

 Okay, I thought. She's just angry

"So why don't you… &*$£ ****, you little &*!?£"

Well, that was a bit harsh.

"And while you're at it, you can keep your ****** nose out of my £$%*&* business or else I'll ****** your ****** skull!"

Oh, come on!

However, I was still staying put on my log. Lemony changed her approach, looking around for something in the sand.

"What did you say about sticks and stones?"

She threw a large stone that hit my log, narrowly missing my leg.

"Hey, you nearly broke my bones!" I cried.

She finally seemed to have got most of the anger out of her system, so we sat a while in silence.

Eventually, I spoke.

"You know, for a while I thought it was Ella rather than the Sugar Tots girl with Stijve."

"I told you that she had a headache," replied Lemony, this time with less spite in her voice. "You aren't the only one capable of telling the truth, you know."

"I know," I answered. "I jumped to the wrong conclusion that she might have been making an excuse. They do look very similar."

"Hmm," grunted Lemony, casually stirring the sand in front of her with a stick. After a long pause, she added, "Why did you do what you did tonight?"

I thought about it. "Because it was the right thing to do."

We sat together for another ten minutes just listening to the lapping waves before Lemony spoke again.

"Okay. I've calmed down now. Perhaps it's time to go back to the apartments. We don't want the ginger prince crying because you aren't there, do we?"

We got up and walked back together, however, I steered her in a different direction away from the stairs we usually took. She frowned in confusion as I led her towards the lift that I'd found earlier.

Guing oop, it announced after the doors had closed. Lemony closed her eyes, shook her head imperceptibly and smiled to the extent that it was almost a tooth-baring smile. I smiled too.

We got as far as the doors to the apartments and were about to knock when she stopped me. She put her hand on my shoulder and said quietly,

"Thank you, Neil."

I glowed.

*

"She's gone!" wailed Stephen. "They're leaving for the airport at four in the morning. I can't believe we had to say goodbye tonight."

His eyes were red from crying. I don't know how long he'd been back, but Mike and Diana had let me in and sent me straight to our room to console him.

"I'm sorry, mate," I said. "Is there anything I can do to help?"

"Nothing," he sobbed. "I'm unconsolable."

I thought of telling him that the word was inconsolable, but I wasn't sure that would help under the circumstances.

"We had such a lovely evening together," he managed to say after he'd calmed down a little. "A moonlit walk along the beach, endless snogging – actually, I think I've sprained my jaw – and we even managed to find a few topics of conversation. I've worked out that not only does she not like Dungeons and Dragons; she also hates Star Wars, all super hero films and has never made anything out of Lego. Oh, and she doesn't live in a pyramid."

His lip wobbled a bit again.

"I'm sure I've heard somewhere that parting is such sweet sorrow. Do you think I'll ever get over her? Perhaps I'm like one of those macaroni penguins, you know, that species that mates for life."

"You're not a macaroni, you noodle," I joked.

We both laughed a little and then a lot. Once we'd calmed down, Stephen asked if I'd been really bored without him and just had a quiet evening.

His jaw dropped lower and lower as I explained everything that had happened this evening.

"Woah, mate!" he exclaimed. "I'm sorry I wasn't there to help you. I feel so bad that I left you to deal with that on your own."

He reflected a bit more.

"Oh yes," he added. "I remember now. As I was coming back up here, I saw Stijve staggering around. I thought he was drunk, but he was clutching his pods at the same time, so it must have been after Lemony had delivered the fatality. Anyway, he wobbled his way too close to the pool and fell in. Two guys who work at the hotel fished him out and dragged him off towards the reception area. I couldn't hear exactly what they were saying, but they were giving him a right mouthful."

We chatted a little more, but by now, it was pretty late, so we changed and brushed our teeth. I think I was asleep the moment my head hit the pillow.

My dreams couldn't have been more eventful than the reality of the night before, and I slept very soundly. I woke up refreshed and ready for the final morning before we had to head to the airport after lunch. Swinging my legs out of bed, I noticed something on my bedside table that hadn't been there the night before. It was a brand new pack of Marvel playing cards placed on top of a piece of hotel note paper on which the single word *Thanks* was written. I recognised my sister's handwriting.

*

Our final morning by the pool was just the way it had been on the first day. Stephen and I were in the water as much as possible, making full use of every minute.

"I am strong when I am on your shoulders!" I sang loudly standing on Stephen's shoulders and holding on to his hands for balance. "You raise me up…"

A soft ball struck me on the side of the head, and I fell off Stephen into the water with a mighty splash.

"Not that strong, eh?" called Lemony from the side of the pool. She was standing there in her yellow bikini smiling down at us. "Come on, kiddies. The mummies and daddies have decided it's time to go, so out you get."

"Jeez, your sister is a goddess!" whispered Stephen to me as Lemony turned away. "Do you think she realises who the best Stevie is now?"

"I thought you were heartbroken about Shamone!" I exclaimed.

"Well, let's not dwell on spilt milk," he replied. I've had time to think things over, and we haven't got a chance. I need someone a bit closer to home if you know what I mean."

A soft ball struck the back of Stephen's head. We turned.

"I can still hear you, you know," called Lemony. "Now,

out of the pool!"

Stephen looked back at me and raised his eyebrows twice. "I think she's interested," he said.

I shook my head in despair as we pulled ourselves out of the pool.

Our holiday in Cala Plata had come to a close.

CHAPTER 19

REPORT TO SCHOOL

Lower Piercing did not seem quite so exotic after Majorca, but it was home.

Staying up later chatting with Stephen into the night was adventurously different, but snuggling into my own bed with my own routine just seemed right.

Mum and Dad had to go back to work of course, so that left Lemony in charge of me during the day. She had also gone back to normal, usually telling me to 'bog off' if I attempted to speak to her. Sure, it was rude, but that was my sister. Her lack of interest meant that the remaining days of the school holiday could be spent with Stephen, Cameron and Grub who were also back from their respective holidays. Grub had loved Jordan and was as tanned as a conker. Cameron had loved his time on the Isle of Iona and was as pale as a ghost in comparison. The sea temperature being a bracing twelve degrees on average didn't stop the Dufresne clan enjoying (or was it enduring?) a daily early morning swim.

We rode our bikes around the village when the weather was good, picnicking under our tree by the river and swinging out on the rope swing while avoiding the notch of course. Most of the time, however, was spent playing the new Dungeons and Dragons adventure that Stephen had got me for my birthday, Danger at Dunwater. It was my adventure, so Hendel the Half-elf was taking a rest. Stephen was still the Archmage, Cameron's Sicosta the barbarian was now experienced enough to cause some serious damage, and Grub had passed the Dungeon Master duties to me in favour of playing a mighty dwarf who had magical *eye-glasses of far-sight* on his equipment list. Looking at our small bespectacled friend, it was clear to see that he was playing a powerful version of himself, but why not?

We had been playing in the lounge at my house one day, and, just as we were breaking for lunch, Grub looked down at the biscuits that were still untouched on the plate next to him. The rest of us followed his gaze and were solemnly silent for a moment. If Wilberforce hadn't moved away, we all knew that those biscuits would have been long gone.

"It's not quite the same without him is it?" I said.

"No," answered Grub. "I'm in danger of gaining a few grams in weight without him to eat my snacks for me."

"And getting through this quest without Geoffrey Pantsniffer to set off all the traps is not going to be as exciting," added Cameron.

"To Wilberforce!" exclaimed Stephen, raising his cup of squash in a toast. We all raised ours and echoed his salute.

Heading out of the lounge to eat in the kitchen, I noticed that the post had arrived and was lying on the doormat. I brought it through but was surprised to see my own name on one of the envelopes – I never got any post apart from around my birthday.

"I've got a letter," I announced to the boys at the kitchen table while they were opening the sandwiches they had brought.

"Ooh. Let me see," said Stephen, taking it from my hand. "Look. It's from school," he said pointing at the franking stamp mark. "A letter from school? You know what that means, don't you? You're a wizard, Neil."

"Well, in that case, give it back, Ron!" I joked.

Stephen laughed and slapped it into my hand before tucking into his cheese, sausage and brown sauce sandwich, the artisan's choice apparently.

I opened the letter up and read it to myself.

"Well. What does it say?" asked Grub.

"It seems that there are some roles of responsibility for year eights, and I've been chosen as one of the pupils to take a role," I read, taking a roll and biting into it.

"Congratulations," said Cameron. "I wonder if any of us have got a letter too. Does it give a list of names?"

"No," I answered, scouring the letter. "It just says that there are six of us, and I have to report to school on Friday at ten o'clock to sort out who gets which job."

"Well that's not mindful of very our quest schedule, is it?" exclaimed Stephen. "We should have been destroying orcs and finding treasure on Friday."

I pondered whether it was an honour to be chosen or a poisoned chalice in that I'd have to give up some of my break times to do a duty. That same thought also made my think that a poisoned chalice would be a good piece of false treasure to drop into the adventure somewhere.

*

"Welcome, Master Peel," announced Mr Campbell as he ushered me into what was my Maths classroom of last year. "I trust you're having an enjoyable summer. You will be in my form, 8C this year so this will be your form room. Please take a seat."

He and I had temporarily bonded over a bad haircut last year, and I thought of that again as I looked at his thick dark hair which was greying at the edges. Like most Maths teachers, he wore glasses and always wore a smart suit. He wasn't everybody's favourite, but I was pleased that that I would be with him this coming year.

It turned out that none of Stephen, Cameron or Grub had been selected in the group of six. Vijay Jayasuriya was already in the classroom along with two girls who had been in the other year seven class last year, Rose Plant and Daisy Melesi. I went to sit with Vijay, giving him an awkward cross between a handshake and a high-five in the uncomfortable way that twelve year olds do. We made brief small talk, mainly wondering about who the remaining two would be and which jobs would need doing. We joked that it felt as if we had won a golden ticket and were waiting to see if Augustus Gloop or Verruca Salt might walk through the door.

As it turned out, the next arrival was a girl called Bella Vochay, a girl who had been in 7D with me last year. I didn't have much to do with her except that I knew she had a beautiful singing voice and could sing in front of the whole school in assembly seemingly without any nerves at all. You could say the same about Mike Prince in the Prince Albert karaoke bar (the no nerves part), but there was a huge gulf in the quality of the voice. Bella sat with the other girls, and after a further five minutes, Mr Campbell came in with a boy I didn't recognise. This boy even held the door open and waited for Mr Campbell to go through first. He was dressed very smartly in the Titfield school uniform, but hadn't been at the school last year; the rest of us were in our home clothes. His straight blond hair was swept across the top of his head in a perfect parting to frame his piercing blue eyes. He glanced at the girls, who visibly blushed and shuffled in their seats, before approaching them and shaking hands with each one in turn and introducing himself. They continuously tucked their hair behind their ears and fiddled with their sleeves. He shook hands with Vijay too, announcing himself as

'Damian Devlin'. He was just about to get to me when Mr Campbell started to speak. I reached out for a handshake, but Damian turned around, ignoring it and sat down next to me, looking forward to pay full attention to the teacher. Fair enough.

"It may seem strange," began Mr Campbell, "to put a new boy into a position of responsibility straight away, but let me assure you that Master Devlin has an exemplary record. He was a prefect at his primary school and has glowing references from his previous school, Eightoaks in the south of England, a private school no less. He was captain of all of their under 12 sports teams as well as earning consistently high exam results."

Something about this information sounded familiar, and I was just trying to work out why when Mr Campbell then explained to us that there were six roles of responsibility for Year 8 pupils and that we had been selected to fill them. They were: music, lunch hall, library, sport, activities, and morning attendance. I couldn't see a great deal of joy in any of these.

"Sir, do we have to do one of these jobs?" I asked. "Surely you had some reserves."

"Master Peel," he replied. "It is an honour to serve your fellow pupils and your school. Let's not start the year on the wrong foot, eh? There are no reserves. At least, not among the boys. There were plenty of responsible girls, but it was decided to give the roles to three boys and three girls."

"I don't mind at all," I said. "I'm all for the best person getting the job regardless of sharing it out."

"Mrs Rees, the Headmistress, has decided," he said plainly. "It seems that your sister, Miss Peel, did so well in her school report last year that it is felt that you are sure to be made of the same stuff and therefore worthy of a role."

Lemony! She'd stitched me up again, this time without even realising it. I did not look forward to her reaction if she found out that she'd had a hand in my new responsibility. However, Mr Campbell's tone was clear. I would not be able to duck this.

My mind raced through the tasks to think which would be the least work and the least intrusive into my day. Would there be any of them I could give up part way through the year just by simply not going?

Before I had chance to reach a conclusion, Bella Vochay had already bagsied music which was fair enough given her singing abilities. Daisy Melesi volunteered for morning attendance which also made sense since her mum was a teacher, Mrs Melesi, and so she was always in early enough to spot who was arriving late. Vijay, who loved his food, put his hand up for lunch duty, probably in the hope that he'd get to eat early when the choice was best or perhaps even get a few treats. This left library, sport, and activities, but Rose Plant quickly snatched up activities. On the one hand, I was disappointed because I'd figured that activities would run themselves after the initial setup. However, at least Rose took part in many activities while I offered diddly squat on that front.

Sport or library?

My dislike of team sports was second to none, and having to take part in a single football match last year was one of the low points of my Titfield career so far.

"Well then, Master Peel, Master Devlin," enquired Mr Campbell. "We have sport and library remaining. What's it to be?"

Damian looked around at me with a thin smile.

"Which would you rather do…er, sorry. Peel, is it? I didn't get your name?"

"Neil Peel," I answered. "Well I hate all sport with a passion, so it's the library for me, I suppose."

"Very well," began Mr Campbell. "Master Devlin on the sports fields and Master Peel in the library with the revolver."

Behind his glasses, he smiled at his own joke and started to make a note on his sheets of paper. Damian was still looking at me with that thin smile.

"Actually, sir," he interjected. "Would it be okay for me to take the library role?"

"What?!" I exclaimed. "But I just said..."

"It's just that I've already been the captain of sport for so long," continued Damian, "I don't want to get pigeon-holed, you see? Coming to Titfield was a chance for me to try something new, and I do love reading; I've covered most of the classics already, Geoffrey Dickens, Blyton, the complete Frank Beans. I think it could give both of us a chance to try something new, don't you agree, Neil Peel?"

"No. I do not!" I protested. "I just said that I hate sport..."

"Calm down, Master Peel," said Mr Campbell. "Master Devlin is new here, so we'll go with his decision. You get sport."

I tried to see if anyone else would swap with me. Daisy Melesi might possibly have been willing to trade, but my school bus didn't get in in time for me to be able to do the early duty. I looked imploringly at Vijay who was keen on sport, but he had convinced himself that food was the correct option for him. He shook his head almost imperceptibly and looked away. I was cornered.

"Fine!" I cursed. "I'll take sport, but this does mean, of course, that my year has been ruined before it's begun."

"Don't worry, Neil," soothed Damian. "I'm sure that a bit of sport won't hurt. You'll face many more serious problems than that this year. I guarantee it."

With that, he reached over to place his hand on my forearm, his thin smile spreading to become a malicious, broad grin.

I snatched my arm away in anger. Who was this boy? Was he trying to wind me up? How come he was so confident before he'd even met anyone else in the school?

Mr Campbell made the adjustments to the plans and explained that we had to report to the relevant member of staff within the first week of term to find out what our responsibilities would be.

I felt hot and so went to the bathrooms to splash some cold water on my face before leaving. As I pushed my way through the school doors, I noticed Damian Devlin sitting on a low wall in the car park. He was looking in my direction with that smug, thin smile still on his face.

"See you next week, Neil Peel!" he called over to me.

I hurried on past. I had faced Basher Walker and Batesy and outwitted them. I had taken down Stijve Tepels, who was probably an adult, single-handedly. I had even managed to put up with Lemony for twelve years. Damian Devlin wasn't going to be able to get under my skin. Why he seemed to be interested in me, I didn't know, but he couldn't spoil my year.

Could he?

THE END

ABOUT THE AUTHOR

Ben Dixon is a father of four children, teacher of French and the author behind the world of Neil Peel. He grew up in Yorkshire, grew up a bit more in Leicestershire before moving to settle in Surrey. *Neil Peel's Holiday* is his second book in the Neil Peel series, following on from *The Heroic Truths of Neil Peel*. He lives in Guildford with his wife, Sarah, and children, Sophie, Isabelle, Max and Kiera.

Printed in Great Britain
by Amazon